SEWING UP SOME LOVE

Indiana Romance 1

Leanne Malloy

Sewing up Some Love
Leanne Malloy

Paperback Edition

CKN Christian Publishing
An Imprint of Wolfpack Publishing
5130 S. Fort Apache Rd. 215-380
Las Vegas, NV 89148

Paperback ISBN: 978-1-64734-541-9
Ebook ISBN: 978-1-64734-540-2

SEWING UP SOME LOVE

Acknowledgments

My husband, Bill, and my daughter, Katie, deserve all my thanks for their support of this book. Bill has always encouraged me to devote time to my writing, even when he wondered what was taking so long! Katie was a patient reader, helping me sort out numerous details in the book.

My parents, the late Reno Foli, and Adele Foli, instilled a love of learning that has endured throughout my life. My sisters, Margaret Conway and Karen Foli, are my best friends and cheerleaders. Cathy Carpenter and Pam Curry fill the roles of "sisters from another mother," proving that time and distance cannot lessen the bonds of friendship. I am forever grateful for God's blessing of loving family and friends.

Prologue

Lauren Gardner pushed a wisp of her wavy hair out of her eye and looked at her finished product. The rose-toned silk jacket had an unusual accent – two raw-edged canvas patches on the front left side. Each patch had a cluster of sequins in its center, giving the jacket a whimsical feel despite the luxurious fabric. The antique pearl buttons, worth a small fortune in babysitting money, completed the look.

Not bad for intro Consumer and Family Sciences, she thought.

Arching her brow, Lauren studied the other class members, all senior males who had deferred their "home ec" requirement. Since she was the only senior interested in advanced tailoring, she was taking the class as an independent study. Most of the guys were hunched over sewing machines and worktables, muttering as they tried to finish threading elastic through the waistbands of their flannel pajama pants. Lauren grinned to herself as she put the last stitch in the final sequin.

Bryan Dawson, in all of his handsome glory,

sauntered over to Lauren's table. "Looks good, Lauren," he said. "Maybe someday you'll work for me at the department store."

Too bad you're so cocky, she mused, grinning in spite of herself. Your snotty personality overshadows your great looks.

Bryan was an heir to the Mohr Department Store fortune which included a large retail store, a chain of restaurants, and a few start-up small business ventures. He, like the others in the class, had put off the CFS course until his last semester at Gordon High. He was the perfect foil for Lauren's dark good looks. Her thick chestnut hair, hazel eyes, and petite frame contrasted sharply with Bryan's blond hair, blue eyes, and six feet of muscular body. Since he was a multi-sport athlete, he trained year-round and it showed.

Lauren had dated several of the boys in her class during high school but never Bryan, which she regretted. She sensed that behind his bravado was a lonely and perhaps insecure, young man. Lauren noticed Bryan's tension when his father, Tom, lectured him after each football game, no matter how well Bryan had played. And his mother, Sally, rarely attended Bryan's events, stating charity functions demanded her presence on most weekends.

"Whatever," she said to Bryan. "My goal is not to work for someone who can make lots of money off of my original ideas, while paying me minimum wage."

He laughed and said, "Come on, Lauren. You know Mohr's pays better than anyone in this town."

Then he became thoughtful. "Why don't we have lunch sometime and talk about this stuff? After

August, we probably won't see each other much." Bryan planned to attend Vanderbilt, a family tradition, while Lauren was staying local for her college degree.

"Sure, that's a good idea," she responded, secretly pleased. "Where and when?" Plans were made to meet at the newest member of his family's startups, Burger Hut, for Saturday at noon.

Saturday was warm and sunny. The leaves on Gordon's sycamore trees were a vivid green, accented by groupings of assorted spring flowers. Lauren dressed carefully in a lilac tank top and beige denim skirt, accented with a tie-dyed scarf. And she waited and waited for Bryan to appear. After two hours, she left, feeling foolish and famished.

"Figures," she muttered, shaking her head. "Why do I care so much about that arrogant jerk? He really set me up."

Chapter One

Ten years later

Scrambling to make it to Jenny's on time, Lauren looked at herself in the rearview mirror as she sat in her car. Makeup: okay. Outfit: casual but professional, therefore perfect for work, which is where she'd been for the last nine hours. Demeanor: irritated.

Why did Jenny's fiancé, Bill, have to choose Bryan as best man? Surely Bill had closer friends than his cousin. The choice meant that she and Bryan would be paired throughout the wedding preparations and festivities. Not that she was one to hold grudges, way back from high school, no less. But still.

I can handle this, Lauren thought. I'll treat him like a difficult patient. I'll stay calm and unruffled.

The aroma of grilled steak greeted her as she entered Jenny's apartment. Jenny was busy in the kitchen, so Bill offered her a drink and appetizers.

Bryan was already seated in the most comfortable chair in the room.

"Just something cool to drink for now," Lauren said. "Work was hectic and I had lunch at three o'clock. I'm still pretty full."

"So you're a social worker?" Bryan asked when she sat down with the iced tea Bill had offered. "Why would you want to work so hard for so little money? What happened to the great dress designer?"

And that's his effort to be charming, she thought, gritting her teeth. As always, his terrific looks take second place to his sense of superiority.

Her response wasn't much better than his question. "I guess my parents didn't work hard enough to leave me their retail empire. I missed the luck of that draw."

As the evening progressed, Lauren and Bryan eyed each other like opponents across a boxing ring instead of two people who loved the bride and groom. Lauren noticed the dark circles under Bryan's eyes; maybe she wasn't the only one with a difficult job. On the other hand, how tough could it be to work for your father? Gordon's only full-service department store held prime retail space on Main Street, offering the sole option for shoppers in their small town. Bryan's job didn't seem all that taxing.

After dinner, they walked to their cars together and Bryan asked, "They're a great couple, don't you think?"

"They truly are," Lauren said. "Jenny's one of a kind. I know I'm biased but she's been my best friend forever. Bill seems to cherish her."

"Cherish. There's a word only a woman would use."

Lauren decided to be the bigger person. "Must be all the wedding vow talk," she said mildly. "Whatever word you use, there's no doubt that they'll be together forever."

"Point taken," Bryan replied. "I want the best for Bill, too. We're more like brothers than cousins. Sounds like you and Jenny have the same kind of relationship that Bill and I do. Have a good evening, Lauren."

As she drove home, Lauren replayed her conversation with Bryan. His looks had matured since high school and Lauren had to admit that he was even more handsome. He had fine lines crinkling at his deep blue eyes when he smiled. Honey-colored hair, which looked blond in strong light, complemented his eyes. Even though he worked long hours at Mohr's, his physique looked like that of a professional athlete. In her car, undistracted by his piercing eyes and sheer masculinity, she realized that Bryan's feelings for Bill were genuine. But that didn't discount his rude assessment of her career. Good thing she didn't hold grudges. Laughing out loud at her own pettiness, she pulled into her garage, thankful that the evening was over.

The atmosphere in the school auditorium was tense and the temperature uncomfortably cool. Clients had been waiting longer than usual for their food pantry orders to be filled. The furnace in the old school wasn't keeping up with the unseasonably cold September winds outside. The metal chairs were frigid as well, and children had begun running between them, chasing each other and irritating the tired food pantry clients.

Spending Saturday mornings in an empty school building sure adds to kids' hyperactivity, Lauren thought.

She wrinkled her forehead and called to Jenny. "What's going on in canned goods? Wait times are over an hour out here." She brushed a lock of hair from her face and, in the process, smeared orange juice concentrate on her forehead. Her jeans were stained with melted ice cream, completing her grungy look.

"Sam dropped a big can of peaches on his foot and we've called his wife," Jenny responded. "We're catching up now that I've pulled Ron from the baked goods area."

Jenny was short, blonde, and bubbly, almost a caricature of the ditzy blonde stereotype. Her innate intelligence was often masked by her carefree approach to life. She was dressed as casually as Lauren, in faded jeans with a T-shirt that read "Bread is life and boy am I living!".

"Great. In addition to the freezer going out, we have an injured helper," Lauren said. "This volunteer job is as stressful as my usual gig!" Despite her rushed words, she smiled and thanked Jenny for her quick thinking.

Lauren circulated among the clients, explaining what had happened, finding understanding and gratitude from most of those waiting. While the people in the auditorium included regulars who came every week without fail, there were also many new clients. Lauren listened sympathetically as she heard stories of layoffs, divorces, foreclosures, and health problems. Her experience when dealing with her father's unemployment years ago, in addition to her training as a social worker, helped her relate well to those needing help from the food pantry.

One man, in his mid-thirties, was especially frustrated. He was dressed in a faded navy blue suit, white shirt, and a carefully knotted paisley tie. "I've been here almost two hours and I'm missing my bus to a job interview," he complained loudly. "What does it take to get a little food?"

After introducing herself and again explaining the delay, Lauren offered the man, Scotty, the option to leave and pick up his order later in the day. He accepted gratefully and hurried off to the bus stop. Other clients whispered about special treatment which required Lauren to again explain the policies of the food pantry. The opportunity to work was primary and the disgruntled clients agreed.

The rest of the morning went smoothly and by noon clients were on their way. The auditorium had been swept and the chairs were rearranged for the afternoon's PTO meeting. Sam's wife called to report that his x-rays were negative for fractures, which was a relief to the volunteer staff.

Lauren and Jenny left and pondered where to eat. Saturday lunch was their reward after each week's stint at the pantry. Jenny hesitated and said, "Lauren, I'm not up for anything pricey today, okay?"

"Sure, but it's not like we break the bank with our weekly lunches," Lauren chuckled. "What's wrong?"

"Bill's mother called again last night. She insists

that because we are paying for the wedding ourselves, Bill and I are disgracing her in front of her friends. Of course, she wants the best of everything and it's just not our style."

"It means a lot for you and Bill to cover the wedding expenses, doesn't it? But there could be worse problems than having Mavis help out!"

"I know I sound ungrateful but you know Mavis has always looked down on me. She keeps bringing up my mom's factory job and how it's a pity my father was never around."

Lauren sympathized with her friend. Jenny's mother had worked hard to provide for Jenny and her brother ever since their father had left them. Both children had grown into hard-working and stable adults.

"Mavis is something, alright. She strikes me as pretty insecure, Jenny. How can she not realize what a great wife you're going to be for Bill?"

Tears welled up in Jenny's eyes. "I don't care how insecure she is! She's hateful."

Lauren grew more concerned. "Jenny, what else did Mavis say?"

Jenny swallowed hard. "I showed her the dress I ordered from Discount Brides and she said it looked like something from a trashy reality show. She went on and on about Bryan's taste in clothing and how I'd be disgracing Mohr's with my dress since it was nothing like he sees on his buying trips for the store."

Bryan's taste in clothing? Lauren wondered.

Her limited contact with Bryan Dawson since high school had cemented her opinion of him as quite a snob, though he had shown some warmth after the dinner at Jenny's a few weeks ago. Poor Jenny. She had a whole new family of pretentious, high-class types to deal with. Not exactly a good way to start a marriage.

"That's really mean," Lauren responded. "How did Bill react?"

"I haven't told him but the dress is ruined for me now. Where can I get a gown on my budget that will ooze class?"

"Good question," Lauren said with concern. "But for now, I'm starved. Let's do the dollar menu at Burger Hut and we'll tackle your wedding budget."

Lunch turned into a three-hour venting, weeping, and counseling session as Jenny detailed Mavis's snide comments during the months she and Bill had been engaged. According to Jenny, Mavis ridiculed her modest engagement ring, the plans for a pasta buffet reception, and, in more elaborate detail than before, Jenny's preferred wedding gown. The dress had been crafted of white polyester satin, with lace appliques featuring pearls and sequins. Lauren was present when Jenny had placed the order and had thought it was beautiful.

The comment on Jenny's ring brought back painful memories for Lauren. Her ex-fiancé, Doug, had made bargain hunting for their engagement ring a laborious, not joyful, quest. He was intent on buying the largest diamond at the cheapest price, his focus on size, not quality. Lauren had loved her 1.5-carat stone and even its flaws were special to her. But Doug had been firm that she was not to tell anyone about the cost of the stone nor its carbon spots, which could be seen with the naked eye if a person looked closely. In retrospect, Doug's attitude was thematic for their whole relationship. Superficial and false.

For a quick second, she thought about Doug's proposal. Despite their previous purchase of the ring, he had made every effort to look like a romantic hero, taking her to a revolving top-floor restaurant in Indianapolis and having their waiter bring her ring nestled in her dessert. Unaware that the wait staff was in on the secret, she was startled by the round of applause, which eventually included all of the customers. Doug had basked in the attention, barely noticing as Lauren put the ring on her finger without his help.

Lauren contrasted her engagement experience to that of Jenny and Bill. The couple had scoured the Black Friday ads last year, setting a firm price limit for the ring. After hours of pre-dawn waiting in line and agonizing, Jenny had decided on a dainty three-stone diamond ring in white gold with baguette accents. The ring represented the couple's commitment to frugality and peace of mind. Jenny was proud of their find and confided that it was a starter ring to serve as a wedding band when she and Bill could afford the larger three-stone band she wanted.

Despite her instinct to jump to her friend's defense, Lauren reacted cautiously like the social worker she was. Family relationships were complex and easily damaged.

"I'm so sorry, Jenny. I wish we'd talked about this sooner," she said.

"It's okay. You don't know how much it helps just to tell you. I suppose I should tell Bill," Jenny said as her voice drifted off.

Jenny had met Bill Sturm in the cafeteria at the regional campus of the state university when they were each finishing their degrees, hers, a master's in education and his, an MBA. According to Bill, he had been mandated by his father to earn an MBA so he could start an entry-level job at Mohr's Department Store, the family business. Without the degree, according to Bill's father, other employees would resent his hiring by his uncle, Tom, the CEO. Bill's mother, Mavis, and Tom's wife, Sally, were sisters, with an unspoken rivalry between them when it came to clothes, appearance, and social status in their small Indiana town.

"Yes, you should tell Bill, Lauren noted thoughtfully. "But I'd couch it in affection and concern for Mavis."

Jenny's blue eyes nearly rolled back into her head. "So you're on Mavis's side now? She's insulted my mom, my taste, and my event-planning skills. And she thinks Bill is marrying down!"

"Yes, she's insufferable. True enough," Lauren said. "But let's tackle one thing at a time. Bill should know what his mother is saying, so that you won't have to keep secrets. You should be full of joy when you're with him."

"Fine, I'll tell him tomorrow when we meet for breakfast. But what about the dress? The wedding is only four months away and I've cancelled the order on the trashy, reality show gown."

"We'll figure it out, trust me," Lauren promised. "Weren't we always going to grow up to have magical powers?"

Lauren and Jenny spent the rest of the afternoon looking at the limited selection of gowns in

Gordon, Indiana's small downtown. They kept open minds, giving consideration to prom dresses, mother-of-the-bride attire, and Quinceañera ball gowns. While no magical powers were discovered, the search served to relieve Jenny's tension and generated much laughter. Jenny's voluptuous figure was trapped in figure-hugging, mermaid-style gowns. The mother-of-the-bride dresses were just that, beautiful, but more suited to a mom than a bride. And current prom gowns left little to the imagination, hardly suitable for a church wedding.

"Just think if I came down the aisle in a hot-pink ruffled concoction, with the front cut down to my waist!" Jenny snorted. "Mavis would turn the same color and faint!"

Monday at work was hectic, as usual. Lauren marveled at the crises that could erupt in two short weekend days. She also wondered at the human capacity for cruelty, something she saw a fair amount of in her role as a clinical social worker at the mental health center branch office. She forced herself to remember the resiliency and kindness she witnessed in most of her patients and each Saturday at the food pantry. Funding for mental health services had been cut again this year, requiring Lauren and the other therapists to fill multiple roles at the clinic.

She observed ruefully that volunteering at the pantry, along with her sewing projects, helped keep her sane. Burnout was a constant threat for those working in mental health. Lauren knew that a balanced life was good protection against that condition.

Her interest in sewing had evolved in part from necessity. After her father's two years of unemployment and subsequent DUI, money had been tight. Early on, her mother, Janice, had tried to make some of Lauren's clothes but the usual result was a tangled fabric mess. Janice's ensuing migraine headache, and the ingestion of a few pain pills, resulted in her mother's long nap and the end of the sewing project. As a result, Lauren taught herself to sew, her skills really taking off once she was in a structured class in high school.

Since then, she had sewn many items for family and friends. Last year she designed an unstructured, alpaca cashmere wool jacket for a local craft fair, selling twelve pieces via the orders she received. The profits helped boost the down payment fund for her small home, in addition to providing a diversion from the stress of her job.

By the time she had dealt with Monday walk-ins, supervision of the case managers, and her two hours of triage, it was four o'clock and she was famished. Deciding that an early supper made more sense than a late lunch, she texted Jenny with that offer. Jenny called Lauren back instantly, full of intense good humor.

"Great idea. The kids have driven me up the wall today. The rainy weekend left them with too much pent-up energy. And Bill's working until nine tonight, so let's eat. Where to?"

"Are we eating cheap, middling, or nice?" Lauren asked, remembering Saturday's lunch.

"Middling is fine. I told Bill about Mavis and he reminded me that our budget wasn't so tight that I needed to be confined to the dollar menus."

Lauren was glad to hear the laughter in Jenny's voice. "How about Melton's in an hour?"

Melton's was one of the few non-chain, full-service restaurants left in Gordon. The menu was varied, with plenty of comfort food options, and was, therefore, a perfect choice for the workdays that Lauren and Jenny had experienced.

After their orders were taken (meatloaf for Lauren and fried chicken for Jenny, with extra mashed potatoes and gravy for each woman), the conversation began in earnest. Lauren took the lead.

"So what did Bill say about his mother's comments?"

"He was irritated but not surprised," Jenny replied. "He grew up with her. He explained that she gets really nervous when she's involved in a public event."

"Public event? It's her son's wedding!"

"I know but Bill said she still competes with Sally. And Sally's parties rival royal functions!"

Lauren sighed. "So Bill understands his mom. Did he have any sympathy about how she affects his fiancée?"

Jenny was thoughtful. "Actually, he was sympathetic. But he also reminded me to focus on us, our goals, and the life we're making together."

"Still, you have a right to your feelings."

"Yes, I know, Miss Social Worker," Jenny teased.

The women laughed together, each comfortable in their long history as friends. "So let's tackle your next dilemma," Lauren continued. "What about the wedding dress?"

"I'm stuck," Jenny wailed, drawing the attention of an elderly couple seated at the next table. "It's too late to order anything in time for a New Year's Day wedding and we can't afford to have a floor model altered and cleaned. As you know, my womanly figure is not going to fit in a sample size four. I thought about going to that place in Connecticut that sells designer gowns at half of retail but I don't have the time or money for the trip. So what now?"

"There's always a solution," Lauren said softly. She was uncertain, however, about Jenny's problem. With so little time left until the wedding, Jenny's impulsive decision to cancel the dress she had ordered may have backed her into a corner.

"Maybe you could look at thrift shops." Lauren suggested. "Or borrow a dress from one of your sorority sisters. You've been in twelve weddings in the last few years."

"No, it has to be my dress," Jenny said with determination. "We'll think of something."

Chapter Two

When she arrived at her house after dinner, Lauren sighed, a mixture of resignation and sadness. She had never imagined that she would be one of those fighting burnout, especially this early in her career. Even her usual evening routine of straightening her 1940s bungalow and planning additions to the décor didn't help her outlook.

Frustrated with her lack of gratitude, she lectured herself as she plumped the sofa pillows. The budget cuts are definitely catching up with me. Time to be thankful for all of the good things in my life, one of which I should be enjoying right now.

Lauren was proud of her home, purchased six months ago after years of frugal living during college and grad school. She appreciated the built-ins, the cozy kitchen, and the fireplace that only smoked on occasion. The larger bedroom had been designated as a master and the smaller served as a combination sewing room and office space. The elegant dining room, the only completely furnished space, was her pride and joy. Her grandmother's cherry table, chairs, and buffet lent a period authenticity to the modest cottage.

The neighborhood was also soothing to Lauren. Her house was nestled among large, stately homes owned by doctors and lawyers. Other smaller bungalows were sprinkled throughout the neighborhood, ensuring a stable but friendly atmosphere. Many of the larger structures were built in the early 1900s, around a huge square plot of ground that was now a park that anchored the neighborhood. Thankfully, Lauren's home was not on the National Register of Historic Places, as many were, so she was able to change the exterior if she wanted. Not that she would paint it pink or add chrome handrails. She loved the sense of permanence in the area. Maybe she was born in the wrong era!

She continued to ruminate. My work is beginning to jade me. Why can't I focus on my many blessings and Jenny's happiness? And why am I turning into a family therapist when she talks about Mavis? Jenny is the most resilient woman I know. She'll handle Mavis with no problems. She just needed to talk things through.

As Lauren chewed the inside of her cheek, she worried about her discouraged outlook. A new pattern of insomnia meant that she was exhausted most days. No matter how tired she was when she went to bed, she tossed and turned for hours. Of course, decreasing her huge caffeine intake would be an easy fix to help that problem. And focusing on the strategies that she preached to her clients such as nutritious food, exercise, and staying in the present, would help immensely with her mood.

But limiting caffeine will kill my career. Without three cups of strong Joe in the morning and then my iced tea all afternoon, I can't function.

The absurdity of her thoughts amused her. Until the breakup with Doug, Lauren had been the poster child for healthy living, exercising almost daily and eating carefully. She was annoyed with herself for letting the end of the relationship affect her this way, "giving away her power," as she would tell patients when they were depressed.

Her cell phone jingled and she was grateful for the interruption. Jenny's voice bubbled through. "Lauren, you won't believe this. I had a brilliant idea about the dress. You can make me a Lauren Gardner original! I'll just tell Mavis that it was a custom creation by an up-and-coming designer!"

After absorbing her shock at Jenny's statement, Lauren sputtered, "Jenny, my designing chops have been limited to christening gowns and holiday costumes. It would have to be a very simple gown. What are your thoughts?"

"Don't use that therapist lingo on me, Lauren," Jenny chided. "My thoughts are something simple and loosely fitted to hide my ten pound weight gain. I'm thinking the fabric should be candlelight satin with a sparkly beaded trim to jazz it up."

Lauren laughed. "Okay, you nailed me. And maybe I could manage something simple. I'll bring some basic patterns over tomorrow. Your assignment is to review all the bridal magazines you've been collecting. Tear out the pages with dresses you like."

"Deal. And I'll have dinner ready for us. Something creamy and rich, I think. Fettuccini Alfredo or Salmon Roulade? You pick."

Lauren thought grilled chicken and a salad would be better for both of them but didn't comment. "Alfredo is good. How about using whole wheat pasta?"

"Ugh. Too gummy," Jenny griped. "But I'll use low-fat milk for the sauce."

Lauren chuckled, feeling better. "Thanks, Jenny. I'm glad we're going to do this."

"I know. You've been so good to support me lately but I can tell you're not yourself either."

"So it shows?" Lauren asked with surprise.

"Yep, but I know you well. You're still in top form at work and at the food pantry."

"Good to hear, Jenny. Working on your dress should be just the diversion I need."

Lauren hung up and wondered if her dark mood was actually loneliness. She missed Doug in spite of herself. He wasn't boring and he had filled the time. Too bad he wasn't gifted with the fidelity gene.

Doug Mathas had been Lauren's first everything: serious relationship, fiancé, and heartbreak. Her initial depressive tailspin two years ago was the result of finding him in bed with his very attractive boss. Despite his protests that the affair was a one-time mistake, Lauren had ended the relationship, much to her parents' relief. They had been quiet, but clear, with their concerns about Doug's constant flirtatiousness, unstable finances, and one-upmanship personality.

After meeting in the graduate lounge at Gordon State, Lauren and Doug had developed an instant connection. It seemed that they had everything in common, though, with time and perspective, Lauren realized how skilled Doug was at agreeing with whatever she said or liked.

The bickering started after a few months and his style changed from agreeable to picky. Nothing Lauren did or said was good enough for Doug's business colleagues, at least according to Doug. In addition, her job at the mental health center, with its on-call commitment and long hours, began to irritate him.

Just before she found him with his boss, they had a fight about her pager. "That stupid thing is chirping again, Lauren," Doug had shouted. "I'm sick of my golf program being constantly interrupted. Get me something to drink and deal with it as quickly as you can. They don't pay you enough for this."

Maybe Jenny's wedding is reminding me too much of what might have been. Or making me admit what "might have been" would have been terrible! With that not-so-comforting thought, Lauren grabbed the latest best seller and went to bed.

After another draining day at work (which included two suicide assessments, an eight-year-old boy acting out in a misguided effort to keep his parents together, and a fifteen-year-old girl with severe anorexia), Lauren's usual pattern would have been to go straight home, and then to zone out in front of her favorite home decorating shows. She was grateful for the chance to have dinner with Jenny instead. The fettuccini sounded wonderful and planning a wedding dress was intriguing.

She drove to Jenny's apartment after work as

promised. Jenny lived in an older building near downtown. Her digs were consistent with her teacher's salary, in that they were comfortable but not lush. One bedroom, a combination kitchen and eating area, and one bath "were plenty for a woman about to be married," Jenny had said when she signed the month-to-month lease. Lauren appreciated Jenny's adherence to her values. She wondered where she had lost her way when it came to Doug's expectations.

"You're here!" Jenny sang out when Lauren rang the bell. "Let's eat first, then we'll plan my 'couture' gown."

Forty minutes and two helpings of pasta later, Lauren felt like a new woman. "Okay, first show me the gowns you like," she commanded Jenny.

As Jenny had indicated yesterday, her favorite choices were simple, both in terms of design and adornment. There were, however, a few strays in the pile of pictures. One looked much like Kate Middleton's elaborate gown and a few reminded Lauren of Kim Kardashian's last wedding concoction.

Ignoring the outliers, Lauren asked, "Jen, these are all lovely but are you sure you don't want a more elaborate dress?"

"No, these are me, elegant without the poufy, wedding cake look. You know I don't want to be a sexpot either. So if we add a simple veil with a headpiece that matches the trim on the dress, it will be perfect." Jenny munched the last of the garlic bread as she commented.

"Great. I think I've seen a pattern that is almost identical to these dresses, with simple cap sleeves, flowing lines, and no defined waist," Lauren said.

She showed Jenny the pattern online, the dress depicted in a bright summer floral print. The lines were simple, as Jenny preferred, and Lauren was happy to see that the dress didn't require a zipper or button loops, details that she would prefer to avoid when working with expensive fabrics.

"Yikes, this is a sundress Lauren!" Jenny fretted.

"I know but look closely. The structure is just like this gown you picked as your first choice. I'd just need to extend a bridal train to the back which is easy. You can decide how long and wide you want the train to be. And when we accent the neckline and hem with the jeweled lace trim, you'll look like a royal princess."

"I guess," Jenny replied. "No offense but is there a way we can test drive this pattern?"

"Sure. I can make a prototype with cheap taffeta and we can adjust from there." Lauren understood Jenny's anxiety, especially given the picture on the pattern. For someone who didn't sew, it was hard to visualize the flowery cotton sundress as a wedding gown.

"Perfect!" Jenny said with much more confidence than Lauren felt. "When will you have it ready?"

The rest of the week flew by. Lauren's caseload was heavy but she was more energized when she worked with her clients. Her evenings were spent eating a healthy supper, then working on the "test drive" gown for Jenny. She had gone to a local fabric store to purchase inexpensive ivory taffeta, which was a fair substitution for luxurious satin.

Lauren enjoyed sewing the simple dress, imagining it in heavier satin with crystal trim along the shoulders and wide neckline. She also bought a few bridal magazines to study current styles in veils. She laughed that the cost of a veil, with little embellishment, could run into the hundreds of dollars. Veils were simple to make. Even silk tulle was relatively inexpensive. She'd have to ask Jenny what style of veil she liked.

Lauren called Jenny on Sunday morning with the news of the trial gown's completion. "Are you ready for the preview?" she teased. "It's sort of like the Golden Globe gown, the runner-up before the important designer dress at the Academy Awards."

"Sure," Jenny replied cautiously. "How does it look?"

"I'll be there in ten minutes and you can answer your own question."

Lauren pulled up to the apartment with garment bag in hand. "Now remember, Jenny, this fabric is the right color but very lightweight. Double-faced satin is heavier and will drape beautifully. The inner seams aren't finished either. They're still ragged. And there's no veil to complete the look."

"Okay, okay, just let me see it!" Jenny squealed. She backed up when the dress appeared from under its cover. "Well, maybe it looks better off the hanger. I'm thinking it looks like my cousin's First Communion dress, suitable for a second grader. That's not the look I'm going for."

"Well, don't worry about hurting my feelings, Jenny," Lauren said with a hoot. "Your reaction is the reason we're trying a cheap sample to start. If this doesn't work, you have lots of other options."

"What options, Lauren? I'm in a bind and I need a dress now! Even buying something off the rack in Indy would be a long shot. I checked online and my only chance is a place that sells dresses on consignment. Their selection in my size looked very slim, unlike me." Jenny slipped on the gown and was surprised by the fit.

"It's wonderful, Lauren. It hangs gracefully, like you said it would. It hides my stomach and I'll be able to eat and dance in comfort at the reception." Jenny was determined to have fun at her wedding, having heard from several friends who had not.

"Do you still like such a simple look?" Lauren asked.

"Yes, I know you're busy but the New Year will be here before we know it. Mavis has been calling daily wanting hints about the dress, too. Now I can say that it has some lace but that's all she's getting from me!"

Lauren was concerned about Jenny's lingering anger at her future mother-in-law. "Have you two been able to talk about the wedding any more? Does Mavis still view this as an event for the community?"

"She's backed off of that for now. I think Bill had a lot to do with it. But I'll admit I've been short with her. She hurt me more than I realized with her comments about my family. I didn't tell you but earlier I was thinking about giving the ring back to Bill until I could deal with her better."

"That's awful, Jenny! You can't give her that much control over your life. If you do that now it will only get worse, especially when you and Bill have kids. Before you say it, I know I sound therapeutic right now, especially given my not-so-great record with Doug."

"I get it, Lauren. You're right. I've been dreading the thought of having kids, which is crazy since I want them yesterday. I imagine Mavis second-guessing my choices for their food, clothing, day-care, and so on. I am giving her lots of power. Or maybe I'm not claiming my own power as a woman. How's that for counselor-speak?" Jenny stuck her tongue out at Lauren as she laughed.

"Atta girl," Lauren said with a grin. She remembered her thought that Jenny was resilient. This conversation was strong evidence of that. She could learn a lot from Jenny in this area. Life was about challenges and she'd already met her share in her twenty-eight years. Lauren realized that she was resilient too, just in different ways than Jenny.

Bill and Bryan came by just as Lauren and Jenny had exhausted their ideas about the wedding dress and the intricacies of dealing with Mavis. Bill's visit was welcome, Bryan's not so much, at least for Lauren.

"Hi, guys," Jenny said innocently. "Bill, did you talk to the caterer about the table linens?"

"Sure did," Bill said. "Though I'm not sure what the big deal was. You'd already covered that with her when we chose the reception menu."

Jenny hugged her fiancé tightly. Lauren and Bryan studied each other in silence.

Bryan was dressed casually but he had an eye for fashion despite his rugged looks. His khaki slacks fit him perfectly, topped off with a charcoal gray, V-neck sweater that showed muscular pecs and just a hint of golden chest hair. Tonight his focus was on the taffeta mock-up on a hanger in Jenny's dining area. "Whose bargain basement concoction is that?" he asked.

Before Jenny could stop her, Lauren snapped back with a quick lie. "It's a Halloween costume for a kid I know from the food pantry. She loves it and she cried when I showed her the pattern."

Shocked by her instant fib, Lauren took a deep breath. At least she hadn't let the secret of the dress slip out. She was also disturbed by Bryan's ability to unhinge her. What was that about?

Bill tried to ease the tension. "Come on, guys, lighten up. We don't want you to fight as you walk down the aisle."

Lauren reconsidered, feeling guilty. "I'm crabby due to a long week, Bryan. Nothing personal."

"No problem, Lauren," he responded quickly. "You're the second person today who has called me out on my attitude. And the first person was my father, so I know I need to look at how I'm coming across. It's great that you're helping the girl at the pantry. I know your job at the center doesn't allow for much free time. Bill has told me about all the people you and Jenny deal with at the food pantry, too."

Lauren looked at Bryan in wonder. Who was this person? He could be very attractive if he kept this up. Maybe working full-time for his dad had forced him to think of others more than himself.

Chapter Three

Lauren's goal of keeping busy was easily met in the coming week. Making the lace dress was more challenging than she had anticipated but the result was beautiful, even with inexpensive lace she purchased from a remnant table. As she finished attaching the two dresses to form one gown, she envisioned a bridal veil trimmed with the scalloped edging of the lace fabric.

A veil in the latest BridalPoint magazine that looked just like that, for five hundred dollars! Maybe she'd been wasting her time on simple jackets and children's clothes. Veils had quite a markup, based on what she was seeing in print and online. On the other hand, designing full-time was not appealing to her. Too many egos to satisfy, too much bending to the whims of the latest fashion trend.

By Saturday afternoon, she was ready to switch her focus from Jenny's gown to her living room project. She dressed for the upcoming task in her oldest jeans, a roomy brown sweater stained with paint from a refinishing project, and her old rubber-toe sneakers. This was her "work on the house" outfit, which always seemed to calm her as she focused on whatever project she was tackling. Today's challenge was a combination of frugality and crafting. Her sofa and chairs were thrift store finds, sturdy, but covered with faded, forest-green plaid. Slowly, Lauren was reupholstering them with heavyweight bargain chintz layered over a base of bleached muslin. She loved the muted floral pattern in tones of blue and rose. The look was very girly but then, who was there to argue about it?

Doug would have objected on several grounds: the feminine pattern, the pastel colors, and the idea that someone else had sat on the furniture before him. Their one attempt at furniture shopping ended in an argument about the pros and cons of free financing, versus paying for what they could afford out of pocket.

As she relived her past with Doug, she tried to stop herself from dwelling on any more painful moments. She powered up the holiday music stream on her cell phone and played jazzy Christmas tunes, which helped her mood. This was yet another thing that Doug would have protested. He hated holiday music being played before mid-December. Christmas jazz in September would have been an outrage!

Lauren was absorbed with fitting the chintz to the sofa cushion when her doorbell chimed. Thinking it was the pizza she'd ordered, she hurried to the door with her purse. As she opened the screen door, she ran smack into Bryan Dawson.

Well, he did look fine. Better than she did, for sure. Obviously, he was coming straight from

SEWING UP SOME LOVE | 31

work. A perfectly fitted, navy blue suit showed his broad shoulders to their best advantage. Fun socks, with dolphins jumping across the space where Bryan's ankles peeped from his slacks, emphasized his chocolate brown shoes, the latest in male trendiness when paired with navy. A pale yellow shirt complimented the dark blue of the suit jacket, causing his eyes to seem the color of the sea before a storm. What was he doing here?

"Leaving because you know it's me?" Bryan asked. "I'm glad I didn't call first and give you fair warning!"

Lauren laughed, her hazel eyes becoming almost aqua green. "Very funny. I thought it was the pizza. Come on in, Bryan. What's up?" She directed him to the sofa, where they sat at opposite ends.

Her casual manner covered her inner discomfort. Bryan's presence unnerved her, which was again a surprise. He looked wonderful, with his dark blond hair brushed back, except for one lock that kept draping over his left eye.

He grinned while he listened to the music playing, showing a small dimple in his cheek that Lauren had never noticed. "Wait, is that Christmas music? It's jazzy, though. I'm sure that's Kenny G on the sax," he said.

"Yep, I'm guilty as charged for violating the start date for Christmas music. Although, these days the holidays pre-empt Halloween. The music helps me focus while I work on upholstery. It's not my best skill set."

Bryan laughed. "To each his own or her own, in this case. Anyway, I wanted to apologize again for the way I sounded on Sunday. And, actually, for a lot of things. Bill has set me straight on what a good friend you've been to Jenny lately. My Aunt Mavis is really something."

"Apology accepted but really, it's not necessary," Lauren said. "Jenny and I have been friends for so long we're more like sisters. She would do the same for me, though I appreciate that you understand how Mavis affects her."

"Yeah, people think the Dawson legacy results in perfect relationships between everyone. In our family, at least, it's more complicated and often full of competition."

Lauren was struck by Bryan's sad tone. "What about you, Bryan? Do you feel you have to compete with your dad?"

"Sometimes," he said thoughtfully. "Tom has improved the store's revenues threefold since he took over. I lay awake at night and know I won't be able to match that, what with all the big box stores and online shopping. And now the major department store chains are adding discount stores to their offerings, sometimes in the same building!"

"I had no idea," Lauren said softly. "It must be hard to feel that no matter what you do, outside forces make success so difficult."

"We're okay for now," Bryan said. "Gordon is such a small town that Mohr's has the advantage since the bigger stores don't feel it's worth their time and money to locate here. And we keep our profit margins purposely slim, to make prices competitive. Lots of customers have told me they would travel to Indianapolis on the weekends to shop if we didn't have such great deals."

"What other strategies have you thought about?" Lauren asked.

Before Bryan could answer, the doorbell rang again and this time dinner was delivered.

"Bryan, can you stay for a thin crust vegetarian pizza? I have a salad in the fridge. I'm trying to stay moderately healthy before the wedding."

"Sure, Lauren. I'd appreciate not eating alone again. Most nights I heat up a frozen dinner. I hadn't realized how dependent I was on Bill for company until he and Jenny got engaged."

"I miss Jenny too," Lauren admitted. "And when she marries Bill, we'll be in big trouble!"

The meal was surprisingly comfortable. Bryan spoke more about the challenges of his job at Mohr's and Lauren was honest about the effect of her demanding career on her outlook. Each was impressed with the other's ability to handle stressful, sometimes no-win, situations.

As they cleaned up the dinner dishes, Bryan complimented her home. "This is a great place, Lauren. Very cozy. Sometimes I get lost in my parents' house. The lake view and watersports are great but seven bedrooms for two people is silly."

"I remember when they built," Lauren said. "The whole town was talking about the Dawson mansion. I had no idea you didn't like it."

"Well, it's good for Tom and Sally," Bryan noted. "It satisfies Sally's need to show off and lets my dad have privacy."

Lauren sensed the underlying bitterness in his comment, amplified by his habit of referring to his parents by their given names. Rather than note this, she tried to lighten the mood.

"I have a bone to pick with you, Dawson," she teased. "You stood me up for lunch at Burger Hut at the end of our senior year. What was that about?"

Bryan was thoughtful for almost a full minute. "Oh, I remember now. My dad chewed me out for making a mistake with the shoe inventory at the store and I had to work all day to fix it. Truly, I forgot about our lunch until that evening and then when I remembered, I figured you wouldn't cut me any slack about it."

Lauren smiled. "You're probably right. I was pretty steamed. And it was a tough time for me with my Dad losing his job and all. I had a real chip on my shoulder. Here's to a more forgiving friendship."

As they laughed, Lauren noticed that Bryan had his shirt cuffs folded under so that they couldn't be seen. Since they were both relaxed, she continued her teasing.

"Is that invisible cuff thing the latest in fashionable men's wear? I've haven't noticed anyone on television with that look."

"Not fashionable at all," Bryan said with irritation. "I popped a button off my cuff and Norma, our alterations lady, is out with the flu. This was my best alternative to a flapping cuff all day."

"Let me fix it for you. I have lots of spare buttons and it won't take a minute."

Bryan took a long look at Lauren and began to unbutton his shirt. Flustered, she scooted to her bedroom and returned with an oversized T-shirt decorated with conch shells and seahorses.

"Here, take this," she said. "It's an extra-large from my last vacation. You can change in my room while I get my notions box."

As directed, Bryan went to Lauren's room to switch to the nautical shirt. Within minutes, she handed him his dress shirt. "I reinforced the other buttons, too," she said. "Really, Bryan, everyone should know how to sew on a button!"

"Well, I guess so. But I think that everyone should know how to hang a ceiling fan. Can you do that?" Bryan's question was accompanied by a sly smile and a wink.

Lauren looked at the handsome man beside her on the couch. His pure masculinity, his strong arms, and the muscles in his shoulders struck her with a force that caught her breath. She looked away and said lightly, "Touché, Dawson. I guess we each have our strengths. If we were all the same the world would be pretty boring. Now go change."

"I really don't need to go to your room, do I? Unless you'd like to come too," he said, with a wicked smirk. He drew the T-shirt off and had his butter-yellow dress shirt on in a flash. Lauren was treated to a quick view of his chiseled chest in the interim and she, again, had trouble breathing. Bryan grinned, probably aware that he was making her uncomfortable.

"I need help with these cuff buttons," he said. "You've sewn them on pretty tight."

"Since you're helpless to replace them, I did sew them on extra strong," she retorted. Lauren buttoned each cuff and as her fingers touched his skin she was again unnerved by the tingling sensation that resulted.

Each stood as Bryan prepared to leave. As he reached the door, he leaned down and brushed her lips with his. "Thanks for the pizza, the company, and the button fix," he said casually. "This was a much better evening than I expected."

Lauren reeled as he walked down her porch steps. What was going on with her? This guy was just an old friend from high school, right? The last thing she needed right now was a complicated relationship with a fantastically good-looking man. She was practically swooning from the great view of his pecs and a simple kiss. She had to get a grip!

After Bryan left, Lauren hummed as she went back to work on Jenny's trial dress. She couldn't focus on the sofa upholstery, having just sat next to Bryan on that very piece of furniture. She put thoughts of his teasing, actually flirting, out of her mind and concentrated on the dress.

The lace overlay looked great and she had scored some discontinued beaded trim to finish off the neckline. The trim had delicate Swarovski crystal beading along with chiffon flowers, a steal at eighty percent off. She carefully basted it on and if Jenny liked it, she would use it on the actual wedding gown. The big test would be next weekend when she brought the finished product to Jenny's house for the final judgment.

Bryan drove home and wondered about the happy feeling he had. Lauren was great company. She was also cute. Actually, she was sexy, he thought with surprise. The sight of Lauren's petite frame enveloped in a huge sweater, along with faded blue skinny jeans, had amused him. Her hair, which had been straight when he saw her at Jenny's, fell into loose waves skimming her shoulders. She was beautiful in spite of herself. Her current look was a far cry from her tailored, nondescript work clothes.

Without any effort, Lauren was as appealing as those models who posed half-naked for the swim-wear magazines each February. He speculated about how she would look in her bridesmaid's dress as she walked next to him at Bill and Jenny's wedding. As he recalled, the bridesmaid's gowns were cut with a dipping neckline. Bryan had no trouble envisioning Lauren's figure in the revealing dress. Her deep brown hair would probably be fancied up into some sort of complicated curly arrangement but he knew that her hazel green eyes would contrast perfectly with the red bridesmaid's gown. She was petite, probably not even five-four, he speculated. He would tower over her when they walked together. He liked that image, of him standing over her, protecting her somehow.

He had also been surprised by the simple femininity of her bedroom décor. A faded quilt, obviously an heirloom, draped the full-sized bed. Coordinating curtains framed the windows, making the ensemble look as though a designer had planned it, in a shabby but sophisticated way. Photos on the dresser showed Lauren and her parents at various ages, in assorted locales, always smiling or laughing. A few shots were of Lauren and Jenny, again with laughter and joy in their expressions. He wondered why the free-spirited woman in the pictures had changed into such a serious creature.

What was he thinking? Lauren was a nice girl but he had no time for a relationship, especially with someone as uptight as she was. He couldn't imagine how anyone could break through Lauren's shell. And what was with that couch of hers? Plaid mixed with flowers? She had mentioned upholstery, he remembered. Good thing he hadn't teased her; she'd had a big needle in her hand after all. But then again, further teasing might have led to more kissing and who knew what else.

But during yesterday's meeting with his father, Tom had made one thing clear: no outside diversions were allowed because the business needed to take priority. Tom had been stiffer than usual, so Bryan knew something was wrong. Needless to say, Bryan hadn't told Lauren about the meeting.

"Bryan, we have to start thinking outside our wheelhouse to reduce our silos or consider closing the store," Tom had announced. Bryan knew when his father starting mixing management metaphors, things were serious. Today's attempt at business parlance was the worst he'd ever heard.

"Our revenues are shrinking," Tom continued, "and customer loyalty isn't what it used to be. More people are driving to Indianapolis to make a weekend of shopping, going to a Colts or Pacers game, and eating at the steakhouses. And lately, Indy has been touted as a new food mecca in the culinary magazines. We're in deep trouble if this continues."

Bryan was caught off guard. "Dad, despite the decreased sales, I thought we were fine. What's changed?"

"Lots of things. The economy is slowly starting to get better and instead of full vacations, people are taking long weekends out of town to shop and have fun. Online purchases are killing us as well. We need a hook to get customers to shop at Mohr's or we're finished."

"A hook? What do you mean, Dad?"

"I'm not sure. I'm thinking we need to emphasize our local charm. We have the river, the historical monument and museums, and our store needs to be a part of this town's culture, just as they are." Tom had looked at Bryan expectantly, almost desperately, as he waited for him to respond.

"Let me think about this, Dad," Bryan said. "It would make sense to get something going before the holidays. The timing is right for a unique slant to the December push. But this is a big project. It could take longer, maybe into the first quarter of the year. I'm glad you told me about all the pressure you're under."

"Good, son," Tom said. "I'm grateful that we're partners."

Bryan noted with a start that his father looked old and tired. Tom's eyes were bloodshot, with puffy circles underneath. His face had wrinkled appreciably since the last time Bryan had taken the time to look closely. His gray hair was still lush but it seemed to lay flat on his head. More significantly, Tom continuously ran his hands through his hair, a sure sign that he was stressed.

"Anything else going on, Dad?"

"No, just the usual with your mother. She thinks I'm made of money and she feels the need to spend it all. Good thing I love her," he said with a wry smile.

Remembering the conversation with his father as he turned in to his driveway made Bryan miss Lauren which startled him. It would be nice to tell her about the actual state of Mohr's and he knew she would keep it to herself, unlike many of the other local women he had dated. When he missed women, it was usually because of their inherent femininity, even their sexiness. What he missed now was a confidante, a partner. Lauren was a good listener and hadn't judged him when he'd confided in her.

He had concerns about trying to save the department store. The other Dawson brands, especially the Burger Huts, were operating at healthy profits. He and his family members could close Mohr's and walk away with an impressive amount of money, enough to last them the rest of their lives if they continued to live as they did now. But Mohr's had too much competition to remain viable in its present state. What "altered state" would work for his family, the town, and the balance sheet? Again, he wished he could bounce ideas off Lauren. Her thoughts, a combination of clinical savvy and pragmatism, might help him identify the core issues of this problem.

On Saturday, Lauren rang Jenny's bell and announced that it was time for the "big reveal."

"If you like this, Jenny, we're going to the fabric store today to buy the satin, lace, and other trimmings."

Jenny slipped on the dress, and her eyes twinkled. "It's perfect, Lauren. I can visualize it with quality satin and Venise lace. But it's going to cost a fortune for those, not to mention all of your time and labor."

"Jenny, I thought I told you. This is my wedding present to you and Bill. And I've got coupons saved for all of the fabric and lace. We're going to get everything at sixty percent off, practically wholesale." Frowning, Lauren looked closely at Jenny. "Jenny, I can't believe I'm accusing you of this but have you lost weight?"

Jenny laughed. "Yep, I've lost five pounds and I hope never to find them. All that healthy eating you've been forcing on me has worked. The dress is a little loose now, huh?"

"Well, we have a couple of options," Lauren mused. "A few of the dresses you chose from the bridal magazines had sashes at the waist. We could add one and you can choose whether to tie it in the front or back. The belted effect will make the dress look fitted."

The two women looked at the pictures Jenny had saved and decided on an organza sash in the palest of reds, to coordinate with the cranberry color of the bridesmaids' dresses. The addition of the sash would make the dress look very similar to the latest design from a trendy bridal boutique in Chicago, popular with brides of all ages.

"Lauren, I love you for all of this," Jenny said tearfully. "It's not just the money you're saving me, it's the loyalty and support that you've given me these last few weeks. And now when Mavis demands to see the gown, I can say it's being custom made, with elements of a DelEzzo design. And before you ask, I made up that designer name!"

"Be careful, Jenny," Lauren cautioned. "You know Mavis will go online and look for that designer. What happens when she can't find DelEzzo? Are you ready for more pressure from her?"

"Don't care," Jenny retorted. "Mavis will have to

stew about it and she can be surprised when I come down the aisle."

After a quick healthy lunch, (grilled chicken salad for both women, with dressing on the side), Jenny and Lauren went to the fabric store for some power shopping. As was Lauren's custom, they first checked the discounted corner for possible bargains. Jenny immediately spied some cartoon-print fleece throw kits, which she declared would be a great project for the children in her class. Twenty minutes later, after an excruciating decision-making process, they settled on three kits, each featuring popular television characters.

"We're here for your gown, remember?" Lauren asked with mock impatience. "Time for the real work."

"What's so hard about choosing fabric and lace?" Jenny asked.

"You'll see. The task of creating something from nothing is laborious!"

At the bridal area, the variety of luxurious silk satins, taffetas, and exotic laces overwhelmed Jenny. Lauren was patient as she educated her friend about the effect of different fabrics and trims on the simple gown they had designed. One trim, featuring pearls, sequins, and three-dimensional lace flowers caught Jenny's eye. She insisted that this replace the trim that Lauren had found on the remnant table.

"It's beautiful," Jenny insisted.

"It's also forty-five dollars per yard," Lauren retorted. "And we need five yards!"

That settled, with the help of Lauren's coupons and an unadvertised sale, the final total for the fabric and lace for the "designer" gown was just under three hundred dollars. They also bought silk tulle and a discounted headpiece for the veil, which Jenny declared was the perfect, simple finishing touch to the look she wanted. Her blonde curls, done in a loose chignon, would blend in with the crystals in the band-style headpiece.

"My gown is going to be absolutely beautiful," Jenny said. "I can see it now. You know what would be a great idea though? How about a coordinating dress for my flower girl?"

Lauren grimaced. "I just can't, Jenny. You're going to have to find a seamstress to help with that. Work is too busy for me to take on another dress."

"Just teasing, pal," Jenny said. "My flower girl already has her dress and it will look perfect with the fabrics we've chosen today."

During the next week, Lauren worked her usual long days at the mental health center and then went home each evening for at least two hours of cutting and sewing. She delighted in the process of creating something unique for her friend and as she worked she discovered that she often came up with creative solutions to some of the clinical dilemmas she was facing at work. The process of losing herself to the gown construction was meditative, helping Lauren relax and stay in the present.

Thank goodness for Mavis and her attitude about Jenny's first dress choice, Lauren thought. It hurt Jenny's feelings but it sure helped bring me out of my blue mood. Working at the center is a good fit for now but, in the future, I need to find a job with better work-life balance.

Lauren thought more about Mavis's reaction to Jenny's original gown. Jenny had said that Mavis barely looked at the dress, just at the price, and then dismissed it for being listed at under one thousand dollars.

What a hard way for a person to live. Mavis could miss the joy of her son's wedding because she'll be focused only on what others would think. At least Jenny and Bill are grounded in their values.

On Wednesday evening, the doorbell rang. Lauren left Jenny's dress out on the cutting table and answered the door. Bryan stood on the porch, looking apprehensive. Despite his tension, he also looked great, clad in slacks and a three-button Henley-neck sweater, which of course, fitted him just tightly enough to hint at the muscular frame beneath.

"I know I should have called but I wondered if you'd be up for some dinner," he said. "I owe you a pizza."

"As a matter of fact I've been working on a project, and I haven't eaten yet," Lauren replied.

Bryan glanced toward the sewing room, observing all the cream-colored satin and lace. "I thought you were finished with the Halloween costume," he said. "And these fabrics are way nicer than what I saw before."

Lauren fidgeted. She hated lying again to Bryan. But she also had to keep Jenny's secret from Mavis's nephew. What rotten luck that Jenny's future cousin-in-law was an expert in women's fashion!

"Ah, well, it's a new project," Lauren said. "Something for a friend who lives out of town. She's going to a fundraiser and with tickets at a five-hundred bucks per couple, she needed help with her dress."

"You're really talented, Lauren," Bryan said thoughtfully. "Let's talk at dinner about that. The store could use some fresh design input."

Really? Just when I thought we had a chance at something more than friendship, he wants to discuss my "talent?" Lauren forced herself to focus as she retrieved her purse and jacket from the closet. Thank goodness she had stayed in her work clothes which included a filmy pink top, tapered black slacks, and nude ballerina flats. At least this time she was dressed for more than upholstery work.

Dinner at The Seafood Dock, located in landlocked Gordon, was delicious and relaxed. Lauren and Bryan both chose crab cakes with Asiago risotto and a pleasant sparkling cider to savor. They shared tidbits about their college years and Lauren was struck by how much she enjoyed talking to Bryan. He then shared his conversation with his father and the dilemma inherent in making Mohr's the first choice for local shoppers. He admitted the store's status was much worse than he'd told her when they'd spoken previously.

"We need a hook, according to Tom," he said thoughtfully. "I just don't know what it could be. Something with local flavor, but unique to Mohr's, would be perfect. And also something priced right, since our customer base is middle-class at best."

"Are you thinking of clothing, locally crafted furniture, a farm-to-table tearoom...?" Lauren asked.

"Not sure, just something that customers will think is worth staying in town, or even coming to town, to purchase. Something special," Bryan responded. "What about your costumes? And the elegant dress you're working on? We could develop a line of budget-friendly clothing designed by a local talent!"

Lauren was both flattered and irritated. She had been having such a good time with Bryan and now his focus was clear. He just needed help with his business. Her presence was for problem solving only. Once again, she'd let her hopes get out of hand and a smooth-talking man was disappointing her.

"I'm not a professional designer, Bryan," she said coldly. "And in case you've forgotten, I have a job that consumes around fifty hours a week, with some on-call responsibilities. I'm not sure how your idea could play out in the real world I live in."

An uncomfortable silence followed Lauren's outburst.

"So I guess we're ready for the check. It's been fun," Bryan said flatly.

The drive home was mercifully short and after Lauren thanked Bryan for dinner she suggested that he keep the car running. She could walk herself to the door.

Lauren barely made it to the door before the tears came. Why does he get to me like this? Will Doug's betrayal always cause me to be this sensitive? Why couldn't I just banter with Bryan about being fed in exchange for business advice?

Suddenly she knew the answer. Bryan could mean more to her than she was willing to admit. Doug had nothing to do with it; she was attracted to and maybe crushing a little, on Bryan Dawson. His devotion to his family, especially his parents, was admirable despite his obvious emotional distance from them. His work ethic was second to none. He had a teasing sense of humor that she welcomed. After Doug's biting criticisms, which he had always insisted were jokes, it was fun to engage in light-hearted back-and-forth volleys. And, obviously, Bryan was supremely handsome.

Great. Attracted to the rich kid, yet again, Lauren fumed. I'm sure not a quick learner. My guard was down and I believed his flattery when all he wanted was to rescue the store.

Bryan pressed the gas pedal hard. What was wrong with her? They had been having a great time, and then she got defensive about her career at the mental health center. Didn't she realize how hard it was for him to open up about the business? Whenever he thought she was warming up to him, she turned frosty. He had no patience for this kind of game playing.

Chapter Four

The arrival of October meant that Lauren's work at the center was even busier than usual. The upcoming Thanksgiving holiday highlighted long-avoided family issues which increased Lauren's caseload by ten percent. She often came home from work after seven, too tired to eat anything other than convenience food and certainly too tired to work on Jenny's wedding gown.

She had to get moving on that dress. The wedding was on New Year's Day. With holiday parties and family gatherings looming, she needed a timeline to stick to or the dress wouldn't get finished.

Jenny also seemed to sense that things were not progressing. She called almost every evening to ask when the dress would be ready for the final fitting. By mid-October, she could take no more of the suspense.

"Lauren, is something wrong with my gown?" Jenny demanded. "I mean, is it turning out ugly or cheap-looking? Mavis is all over me about details and I don't even have vague hints to offer! Not that

I mind leading her astray, of course."

"No, it's going to be beautiful, Jenny. I'm just stalled because I'm so busy at work. I'm thinking about taking all of Thanksgiving week off, so I can finish it ahead of schedule."

Jenny wasn't convinced. "Are you sure it's okay? Why don't I come over tonight with dinner and we can see what needs to be done? If we need to, I can bring it to a seamstress in Indianapolis for the finishing touches."

"Absolutely not!" Lauren barked. "This dress is my creation and no one else's!"

"I'll be there in a half hour," Jenny replied. "And you'd better be ready to tell me what's really going on. I believe you that the dress is going to be fine but there's more to this delay than you're telling me."

Jenny arrived as promised, bearing toasted sub sandwiches. After she and Lauren had eaten, Jenny launched her DA-style questioning.

"So what's going on with you and Bryan? You were happier than I'd seen you in a while, then a couple of weeks ago you were back in the dumps. Did he hurt you?"

"Yes and no," Lauren said quietly. "I had my hopes up, I guess. I thought he might care for me but he just wanted to talk business. He suggested that I could design a line of clothing for Mohr's to provide a local interest slant, to help the store out."

"And that's bad?" Jenny asked, startled. "If you knew anything about Bryan Dawson, you'd know that to be privy to his business concerns, you're something special."

"I don't think so, Jenny. He was only into helping

the business. He's never indicated I'm in any way special to him." Lauren looked away, avoiding Jenny's gaze.

Jenny frowned. "Lauren, I love you, which you know. But you are being a pig-headed fool if you think that you're not special to Bryan. Bill even said the other night that Bryan had been in a great mood until the dinner with you at the Seafood Dock. And, sometimes, I wonder if you got into social work because of your feelings for him from high school. You always said that he seemed lonely and pressured."

"You're making my point, Jenny. He was in a great mood until I said no to his business venture. Let's just work on the dress for now. I need something to keep my mind off Bryan. We sure aren't getting anywhere arguing about him. And for the record, I got into social work due to my dad's problems, not Bryan Dawson's!"

Jenny insisted on a trial fitting as payment for the sandwiches she had provided. With the lace overdress basted in and the beaded trim pinned on, Jenny pronounced the dress a success.

"Whew, I'm glad I got to see it," she told Lauren. "I had terrible visions of something I would have made in eighth grade. It's going to be lovely."

Finally motivated, Lauren sewed with renewed intensity after work each evening. She also basted together the veil and headpiece. The final product turned out to be identical to a veil she had seen in one of Jenny's bridal magazines with a list price of six hundred dollars.

Maybe she did have a knack for this. The beautiful veil made the dress look like a designer gown. She had often wondered if she should focus more on sewing. Maybe she could supplement her income by crafting other items so that she could eventually get out of the mental health center grind.

Lauren also did a lot of thinking about Bryan and her harsh rejection of his offer to design for Mohr's. She felt ashamed for dismissing his idea especially when he had opened up about the trouble that the store was in. Her social worker empathy finally kicked in, having left her when she had dinner with Bryan.

Based on their recent contacts, she realized that Bryan was a good person. Truly good, not sanctimonious, but committed to making life better for others and working hard to save his family's legacy. She felt pulled to him in a different way than in the past. Her attraction was based on tenderness, admiration, and depth of feeling.

Too bad I've blown it with him, Lauren grumbled inwardly. If he had half a brain, he'd be hunting for an heiress to save the store, not a social worker with a home ec sideline.

Jenny visited the next weekend and reminded Lauren about the need to plan her bridal shower. She and Lauren enjoyed compiling the guest list, which Jenny said would be made up of "girls we can have fun with." Lauren reminded her that Jenny still needed to invite her own mom, Mavis, and Lauren's mother, Janice, which would probably put a damper on the "girls having fun."

"Well, if we must," Jenny whined. "They're all great women but we need to cut loose a little."

"There will be time for that at the bachelorette party," Lauren reminded her. "Now what do you think about shower games? Yea or nay?"

"Of course, we have to have the game where guests design toilet paper wedding dresses," Jenny chortled. "Since we've designed the ultimate gown, it will be our little private joke. But other than that, I'm not a big game person and neither are my friends. I'm up for playing relaxing music, telling stories about our lives together, and eating your great cooking."

This led to menu planning, with Jenny requesting several finger foods instead of traditional luncheon fare. Platters of mini quiches, bruschetta, and assorted tea sandwiches comprised the savory dishes. Mints, nuts, and punch were the sweet offerings, including the cake, of course. Jenny asked for a three-layered carrot cake with cream cheese frosting, accented with toasted coconut. The shower date was set for two weeks out, e-vites were sent, and, by the end of the evening, Lauren had twenty acceptances for the party.

"Whoa, that was quick!" Lauren said. "I've spent so much time worrying that I forget how easily things can, and usually do, fall together. That line of thinking is Anxiety Management 101 but I tend to fret anyway!"

"I realize this is all pretty old-school," Jenny said. "But I love the traditional approach to showers and it suits me and Bill. I recently went to a bridal shower that was solely focused on gifts for the couple's pet schnauzer!"

"Yes, weddings are a big business," Lauren said. "I love them though, as long as the couple makes the ceremony their own, like you and Bill are doing. You can always tell when the parents of the bridal couple are running the show."

"You mean like Mavis?" Jenny asked. "Good thing Bill and I were able to calm her down."

Two weeks passed quickly. This November in Indiana was beautiful with the colorful leaves lingering on the trees past their usual fall date. Lauren always loved autumn but this year it had a sad aspect for her. Soon she would be sharing her best friend with Bill Sturm. Why couldn't she cut loose, as Jenny would say, and enjoy dating around or even get on an online dating site?

Ugh. The thought of dating filled Lauren with dread. Since her breakup with Doug, she'd had a few dates, often arranged by friends. While the men were good people, often Lauren convinced herself that she had nothing in common with them. One fellow bragged about his impressive collection of NASCAR memorabilia. Since Lauren was an IndyCar fan, they'd sparred over the two types of racing. She had to admit that she was much too picky. Why couldn't she find the commonality in the competitions instead of rejecting a good man? Because she was afraid of getting hurt again. She wouldn't let that happen.

Her mind went back to Bryan, his blue eyes, and the tense but endearing expression on his face when he talked about the family business. She wished she could help him. But when he asked, she had shot him down. What a hypocrite she was.

Shower day dawned with the inevitable November drizzle. Lauren's house was sparkling. She had used the upcoming bridal shower as motivation to finish reupholstering her sofa set, which filled her with pride. No more pastel floral and green plaid combination. Instead, her welcoming area looked like a real grown-up living room.

She had also found the energy to repaint her small bathroom, which had been a hideous pink when she moved in. Repainting then necessitated the purchase of new towels, rugs, and accent pieces. The effect was just what Lauren hoped for, cozy and complimenting her bedroom decor. Frugality had its place but, sometimes, she needed to create beauty in her home.

Rising early to finish the food preparation, Lauren polished off the carrot cake frosting, silently promising to make Jenny pay for the three-layer requirement. Two layers would have tasted the same and would have been much simpler. Her mother arrived an hour before the shower's start time to help plate the sandwich items.

"Honey, I'm impressed with how nice the house looks," Janice said. "I had my doubts about that sofa and loveseat but they look straight out of a magazine. The bathroom is impressive too. Do you ever sleep?"

"Not much," Lauren admitted. "But it's getting better, now that the stress of Jenny's dress is behind me. Anything new with you and Dad?"

Janice adjusted her necklace and earrings which coordinated with her rust-colored sweater. "Nothing that most other sixty-year-old people don't also deal with," she said. "We've got to lose a few pounds and exercise more. I've been trying out new recipes which taste wonderful but the tiny portions leave us hungry in two hours. Kind of defeats the purpose when we have a snack before bedtime. But we'll figure it out. We always do."

Lauren hugged her mother. "Yes, you guys always figure things out. I could learn from you two."

"There's nothing extraordinary to learn, honey," Janice said, hugging her daughter hard. "God helps us, as you know, no matter what we're facing. Keep praying. Be yourself and do your best. And maybe in your case, forgive yourself for not being perfect."

Guests arrived on time and after the usual pleasantries and introductions, food was set out. Everyone ate heartily. Several women made Lauren promise to email the recipes for the luncheon items. Mavis was subdued and Lauren was pleased to see Jenny chatting with her attentively. Janice helped Lauren with replenishing the food trays and finally everyone was seated for games and gifts.

Lauren teased the crowd. "Jenny and I know how much everyone loves shower games," she announced. "So we've come up with the five most popular games on the Internet. We figure that we'll be through with them and able to open gifts in a couple of hours."

Subtle gasps greeted this and Lauren was quick to admit her joke. "Not really! We've decided on one game only. Split into pairs and decide which of you will be the model and which will be the designer." Relieved laughter ensued and several of the women knowingly nodded and mouthed, "TP."

Toilet paper rolls were distributed and the timer

was set for fifteen minutes. Giggles filled the room as the pairs of women fussed over their creations. A few shrieks were also heard due to pins and staples missing their mark, instead, connecting with skin. After time was up, pictures were taken and voting done on the prettiest "gown." Each of the ten gowns inspired good-natured laughter. One dress literally fell off the model as she walked around the small living room. Another had so much tape and so many staples that it was difficult to remove from its model's own clothing.

To everyone's surprise, Mavis and Janice won the contest hands down. Their gown featured a halter neckline, layered skirt, and gathered "veil" with toilet paper rosettes. They clinched their victory with a detachable lower skirt, turning the creation into a mini-dress for the "reception." Mavis made the ideal model, slowly pirouetting around the room.

"You don't know how much I've enjoyed this," Mavis said later to Jenny. "I needed something to get my mind off of things."

"Are you okay, Mavis?" Jenny asked.

"I'm fine, dear," she replied. "Just lots to think about lately and, of course, I still don't know much about your gown."

"It's a beauty," Jenny said with confidence. "But still a secret."

Mavis frowned but was quickly diverted with the unwrapping of the gifts which took another hour. Jenny was effusive with her thanks to her guests, noting that everything they had given her would be put to good use. The gifts were a thoughtful mix of selections from Jenny's registry, hand-crafted items, and gift cards.

"You are all the best," Jenny said with tears glistening in her eyes. "Nothing can replace friends and loved ones. I can't wait to see you all at the wedding."

After the treasures were unwrapped, the women settled in for more food and chat. The carrot cake was a hit and Lauren promised again to email everyone the recipe, emphasizing that two layers would be just as delicious but with much less labor. Jenny had the grace to blush.

Later, Lauren overheard two of Jenny's fellow teachers speaking quietly about Mohr's. One was sitting next to Mavis who had gotten up to get more punch.

"I hear it's going to close soon," Sarah said. "The new Walmart in Shelbyville was the last nail in the coffin."

Lauren walked over to them. "Really, Sarah? I've heard just the opposite. Mohr's is due for an exciting announcement of some kind." Her lighthearted manner belied her concern about Mohr's. And about Bryan.

Mavis had just returned and she gave Lauren a small smile of thanks. No one else had heard the conversation for which Lauren was grateful. As much as she loved her small town, the constant gossip infuriated her. There were few secrets and if there were, fabrications often took their place in the daily need for things to talk about.

Eventually, the guests began to make their way home. After the house was empty of everyone except Jenny and Lauren, they rehashed the afternoon.

"Well, girlfriend, you didn't do too badly for

yourself," Lauren said, grinning. "Your kitchen is pretty much complete and you've got lots of linens for the beds and baths. You can fill in the gaps with the gift cards."

"Yep, I have way more towels and sheets than I need. But mom says they don't last forever and I'll be happy to have fresh ones to put out in a year."

Jenny continued. "What did you think about Sarah's comment? Is it true Mohr's is doing that poorly?"

Lauren hedged. "Who knows? The news reports say traditional retailers are struggling but Mohr's always seems busy to me."

"I guess so," Jenny said. "Sometimes Bill is quiet in the evenings but he won't talk about what's eating him."

There's a lot eating at him and his cousin, Lauren thought. I wish I had a second chance to help. No, I won't wish for a second chance. I'll make one happen. Bryan deserves better from me.

Chapter Five

Being an only child was both a joy and a burden for Lauren. Her parents' fertility issues would have been dealt with easily today but, almost thirty years ago, Peter and Janice considered themselves fortunate to have one healthy baby girl. Lauren was grateful for their unconditional love. Like most only children, though, she knew she related better to adults than those closer to her own age. Her sense of humor, along with a deep empathy for others' pain, compensated to make her a valued friend and co-worker.

Too bad she hadn't sympathized with Bryan's work dilemma. His obvious anguish over Mohr's difficulties had been overlooked when she assumed he was interested in her only for her clothing designs. Maybe that was another negative factor in being an only child. Was everything always about her? Lauren shrugged off the convicting question but admitted to herself that it bore truth. Her selfishness, her fearful guardedness, and her determination never to be hurt again combined to create a wall between her and others.

60 | LEANNE MALLOY

So I want a relationship, only on my terms, with no risk, Lauren pondered. That's a sure recipe for loneliness. Time to recognize this pattern and make a change. And it's time to be thankful for all the joy in my life. Faith, family, friends, work – who could ask for more?

As was common with most families, Lauren and her parents relished cooking the same Thanksgiving favorites each year. These included slow-roasted turkey, sausage and cornbread stuffing, and pumpkin-pecan streusel pie. The more traditional side dishes were also included. As Janice finished the food preparation, Lauren set the table using the harvest-themed decorations that had been carefully stored away last November.

"These placemats sure carry lots of memories, Mom," Lauren said. "I remember all the years we had Jenny, her mom, and Ryan for Thanksgiving. Those meals, especially when Ryan was little, were crazy but fun."

"We have so many good memories, honey. I'll never forget you and your dad working on your fourth-grade papier-mâché project that was due right after Thanksgiving. Our dining room table was your workspace, so we made Thanksgiving into a picnic on the living room floor. Jenny's brother thought he'd died and gone to heaven!"

Both women laughed as they worked and Lauren spoke again. "You know, Mom, I admire your ability to cherish all the good times. Sometimes I question my faith because the bad times pop into my head lots more than the good ones."

"You're still healing, Lauren," Janice said firmly. "Your faith is fine. What I think you need to pray for is not just positive thinking but the courage to believe there are good men in the world. I believe there's a special man for you, one God will put in your life when you're ready."

Lauren bristled at her mother's words. "So Doug was in my life because I wasn't ready for someone good? I don't get it, Mom."

"You know that's not what I meant, Lauren. This imperfect world is full of imperfect people, us included. The thing we need to pray for is to have the strength to deal with those who hurt us and the wisdom to choose those who will love us." The doorbell chimed as Janice's words hung in the air.

As usual, she's right. I have lots to chew on today, Thanksgiving dinner being the easiest! Give me strength and wisdom, dear Lord, Lauren prayed.

Another Gardner Thanksgiving tradition, since the table was empty with just three people, involved hosting a family from their church. Usually, the family was stranded in Gordon due to a job transfer and lack of funds to return home for the holidays. The year the guests were the Stanfields: twenty-something parents Sam and Elaine and their four-year-old daughter, Courtney. The Stanfields planned to go home to California for Christmas but had to stay in Gordon for Thanksgiving.

Courtney was an independent, feisty little girl. Her choice of holiday attire reflected this. A green T-shirt, purple tutu, and strawberry-printed rubber rain boots combined to create her ensemble. She was also a big fan of Lauren's because Lauren had designed and sewn her christening gown and, most recently, this year's Halloween costume. Courtney had demanded a "princess dress," but insisted that it be made of black satin with appliques of circus animals.

"Obviously, she chose her outfit," Elaine said apologetically as Courtney sashayed around the room. "She said she wanted to wear all of her favorite things for Lauren to see."

Lauren laughed and praised Courtney's selections. "You're going to be a designer someday, kiddo. Keep up the good work. I could use some of your creativity in my designs."

Courtney drew Lauren aside while the feast was being brought to the table. Her brown eyes twinkled as she whispered to her idol. "My friend at school, Nora, taught me a new word. It's very special but we can't say it too much. Want to hear it?"

Lauren, wondering what she was in for, decided to humor the little girl. "Sure, Miss Courtney. What is this special, secret word?"

Courtney leaned forward as Lauren bent close to hear. "It's A-MA-ZIIING. Isn't that a great word? Want to have me use it in a sentinz?"

"Sure, sweetheart. Use it in a sentence."

"The puppy rolled over and he was A-MA-ZII-ING," Courtney said proudly. "I think it means he was smart."

"Wow, you've learned a good word from Nora," Lauren said. "But why can't you say it too much?"

Courtney's whisper grew softer. "Nora loves that word. She even named one of her Barbie dolls 'A-MA-ZIIING.' Nora's mom said if she heard that word one more time, she'd go nuts!"

"Well, Nora's mom probably wants her to learn

other new words. Could that be the reason?"

"Maybe," Courtney said, scrunching her face. "But Nora's mom says nuts A LOT. She needs to learn new words, too."

Lauren admitted defeat as she hugged Courtney. "Looks like we're ready to eat, little one. Do you know how to say the blessing?"

With Lauren's help, the meal prayer commenced. Courtney was proud of herself, especially when she announced, "At Grandma's house, I have to sit with the little kids. Here, I'm big!"

Courtney provided numerous distractions throughout the meal, culminating when she speculated about "why the turkey had dough in its bottom." Sam and the Gardners laughed until they had tears in their eyes but Elaine was mortified as she tried to explain both anatomical and culinary facts to Courtney.

Lauren laughed too but she was inwardly pensive. Sam and Elaine were younger than she was and already raising a little girl. When was it going to be her turn? She hated her feelings of self-pity but couldn't stop them. As she told her clients, "feel your feelings," and then work through them. Change what you can and let the rest go. She shook her head and chuckled at her own therapist self-talk.

When was she going to give it to God for good? She kept saying "His will be done," but she also prayed often for a good man to enter her life. Kind of a contradictory set of prayers, wasn't it? What had her mother said about strength and wisdom? When was she really going to believe that God was A-MA-ZIIING?

After the Stanfields left, Lauren and her father did the cleanup, since Janice had done the bulk of the cooking. While Janice studied the Black Friday ads, Peter and Lauren washed the pots and pans.

"What's the latest in your life, Lauren?" Peter asked. "Is Gordon's most eligible bachelorette having fun?"

"If you define fun as being constantly busy, yes, I'm having tons of fun, Dad," she said. "I'm glad you and Mom can chill a little these days."

"Well, we chill, weigh ourselves, walk around the block, and then we do our budget," he laughed. "Transitioning to a fixed income is scary, even when the figures say you've got enough to last until the end. That's where God comes in, I guess."

Peter Gardner had always been quiet, almost rebellious, about his faith. He frequently said being in nature was the most religious experience he could imagine as he focused on the wonders God had created. He'd often quipped that church made him itch. It was rare for him to talk like this.

"You mean faith, Dad? Mine sure varies, depending on what's going on with me."

"No argument there," Peter said seriously. "When I was laid off, I made some stupid, faithless decisions and now, in retrospect, I see God was with me the whole time. Despite my lack of belief that He would help me take care of my family, He came through, as He always does."

"But how did you do it, Dad? In my profession, we struggle with how to deal with problem drinking." Lauren blushed, hoping the label of "problem drinker" wouldn't offend her father. But then again, he'd fit the bill back then.

"I bet I did the things you tell your clients to do," he said. "In addition to praying and honoring God, I tended to my physical health. Remember how I lost fifteen pounds after the DUI? I decided, with God's help, that I would take charge of the parts of my life that were under my control. I still beat the streets looking for a job but, in the meantime, I exercised, ate healthy, and got back into playing my guitar. In your language, I learned better stress management."

"You know what else?" he continued. "I asked forgiveness for the stupid things I did when I lost my belief in God. Your mom and I had some whopping arguments during that time. She was afraid to trust me again, afraid that my seeking forgiveness was just for show."

"Wow, I remember some of that but I was so absorbed with my own high school drama I never put it all together," Lauren replied. "You're wonderful, Dad. How am I ever going to find a guy like you?"

"You will, honey. And it occurs to me that I need your forgiveness, too. You dealt with a lot on your own. No irritating siblings to offer distractions. No big house to hide away in when your mother and I were arguing. And the embarrassment of a dad who was pulled over for drinking, with the whole town reading about it in the paper. The Gordon gossips were very busy, I'm sure. I'm so sorry, Lauren," he said, choking slightly on his words.

Lauren gave her father a strong hug, saying, "It's okay, Dad. I love you to pieces."

She was struck by his request for forgiveness. It was true that his drinking had instilled in her a sense of fearfulness about the future, of not having enough money, and of wondering what a man would do next when trouble came. In her eyes, though, he would always be the best father in the world. It was odd how she'd come to that place without realizing it. Maybe she could learn to think the best of other flawed men.

Meanwhile, Bryan was dealing with Thanksgiving stressors of his own. His parents had invited Sally's sister, Mavis, and her family for their traditional dinner. China, crystal, and silver flatware combined for a Food Network-worthy tablespace.

The Dawson's lake house was more castle than rustic getaway. The dining room table comfortably seated twelve and, in a pinch, sixteen. Chairs were upholstered in the latest abstract silk shantung print. Open to the dining area was the great room, with a floor-to-ceiling stone fireplace. During power outages, somewhat common in rural Gordon, the wood fire could heat the whole main floor. Tom, Sally, and their boys had enjoyed several overnight adventures in sleeping bags by the fire when power was lacking.

Bryan looked at his parents closely, noting their ease with each other. Tom certainly didn't seem to begrudge the expensive china and silver; he seemed instead to bask in the opulence of his surroundings.

He wondered if Tom was as much a spender as Sally. The elder Dawson often blamed Sally for her extravagance but he didn't put up much of a fight about it either. And Bryan had to admit his mother had great taste. The décor on the main floor flowed seamlessly from room to room, without being repetitive or boring. Soothing colors of ice blue, cream, and light brown permeated everything from the sofas (all three of them) to the stoneware dishes in the kitchen.

Conversation was slow and stilted, more so after an interaction between Mavis and Jenny about the wedding gown.

"I'm concerned, Jenny dear," Mavis said. "You're so secretive and I can't find that designer you mentioned anywhere online."

Jenny was cool and noncommittal. "I know, Mavis, isn't it odd for a hot designer like DelEzzo not to have an online presence? But he's all over the edgy bridal magazines, so I'm trusting the dress will be perfect."

"Edgy bridal magazines?" Mavis asked. "What does 'edgy' mean?"

"Oh, you know, alternative gown colors like red or purple, unlined corset bodices, feathers...." Jenny mused, with a glint in her eye.

Bill looked as worried as his mother. "Red, Jenny? Feathers? And corsets? I just don't know about all that. What will Reverend Taylor say?"

"He'll be fine with it, honey," Jenny said sweetly. "He knows a marriage is built on more than the superficial details."

Everyone focused on their food after that but Bryan wondered about Jenny's cavalier attitude. Last month she had been telling anyone who would listen about wedding minutia. Now she was very secretive.

Something was going on. He wondered if Lauren knew what it was. He would have to find a way to get Lauren to talk to him.

After dessert (pumpkin chiffon cheesecake, catered by the company that had provided the entire meal), Mavis tried again. "And what about the veil, Jenny? Has your designer talked about length, trim, and embellishments?"

"I'm not sure about a veil," Jenny said, again with a twinkle in her eye that only Bryan noticed. "I saw a hat in a magazine, part of a Mardi Gras photo shoot, that intrigued me. It had a huge brim and netting down to the floor. The designer called it the 'bee-keeper' look. It's very fashion forward."

Bill's look of horror stopped Jenny's joking. "I'm sorry, Mavis. I'm just teasing. My veil will coordinate with the dress. The reviews of DelEzzo's wedding ensembles have been glowing."

"Wish I could read some of them," Mavis muttered.

Chapter Six

Black Friday shopping, despite the early hours and hassle involved, was another tradition Janice and Lauren Gardner fiercely honored. Janice's frugal nature had helped her family during many a tough time and now she loved the thrill of bargain hunting.

"It's a game, honey," she said to Lauren. "Why spend more if you don't need to? What's on our list of BF specials?"

"You're looking for a wedding gift for Jenny, a dress for said wedding, and Christmas gifts for Dad. I could use new sheets. Also, some pillows for the couch, in my new color scheme. Forest green plaid with cotton fringe doesn't look good with my pastel brocade," Lauren said.

Plans were made for the most efficient way to find their treasures. The women split up for two hours as each tracked the goals on her list. They met for lunch at the local refurbished diner, laden with bags and wearing tired smiles, indicating success.

As they waited for their turn at the counter, they praised each other's efforts. "As I said, honey, isn't this a fun game?" Janice asked. "Nothing gives me a rush like finding a bargain at seventy-five percent off with a coupon for ten dollars to spend next week."

"Yeah, it's fun," Lauren said. "But it's also work. You've got way more stamina than I do, Mom."

"Well, I'm semi-retired, which makes having stamina a lot easier. What's wrong, Lauren? Is your job going okay? You still seem a little down when we talk. I can tell you're putting up a front for me so I won't worry."

"Fighting a little burnout, I guess," Lauren admitted. "And it's hard watching Jenny prepare for her wedding when I've got no one special in my life. Even the Stanfields, who are younger than I am, have their lives on track. I feel stuck."

"We've got to have faith and trust that God's will be done," Janice said firmly. "God will find you a good man and you don't want to settle. Your professional challenges always seem to work out, don't they? This will, too. Faith needs to be your anchor." Janice left unsaid her firm belief that Lauren had been settling with Doug but both women were aware of the message.

"Mom, it's easier for you to have faith. You don't rely on your job for your living. You've got time off to devote to your hobbies. And you and Dad are in a great place."

"But that wasn't always the case, was it? Dad and I went through a lot of messy experiences. In a way, having time to myself makes faith harder. I'm stuck with my own thoughts in the quiet house and it's easy to lapse into worrying about you, your Dad, and all the unknowns ahead of us. I pray a lot, believe me." Janice's sincerity took the sting out of her preachy comments.

Lauren had renewed respect for her mother. Her mom was right. Faith had helped her through many a difficulty and the future was uncertain for everyone. God's presence in their lives was the only constant.

Lauren called Jenny the next day with a peace offering. "I've been thinking and, as usual, you were right about Bryan," Lauren said. "I've made a mess of it all but it's motivated me to finish your gown and veil. Come over this afternoon for the final fitting and, if all goes well, I'll treat you to dinner. If you don't have plans with Bill, that is."

"No need to apologize, Lauren," Jenny said with relief. "Men can be thick and we forget that sometimes. I knew you'd finish the gown. I'm really excited. I've been having fun telling Mavis that the designer was keeping me in suspense about the finished product."

"That's my buddy, finally getting the last laugh on her future mother-in-law."

Jenny arrived at noon and the fitting was a true success. As Lauren and Jenny compared the dress to the one Jenny had originally picked from the bridal magazine, they agreed that they liked their "designer original" even better. With her heels, veil, and a prop silk floral bouquet from Lauren's living room, Jenny looked every inch the beautiful bride.

"Thanks again, Lauren," Jenny said tearfully.

"You've saved my budget and I love the dress. Mavis will never need to know and even if she did, anyone could see this is a quality gown."

And then, Lauren's newspaper in hand, in walked Bryan Dawson.

"I knocked but there was no answer. What's all this?" he asked. As he looked at Jenny, his face was questioning, then angry, and finally amused. "So Lauren, this is the dress for your friend's charity gala in Indy, right? Jenny, what's going on?"

"Your aunt is what started this but then Lauren's talent saved the day. You won't tell Bill about it, will you?" Jenny pleaded.

"I'm not sure, Jenny. Bill and I play it straight with each other and he's been worried about how you were going to get a dress after you cancelled the original order. You also blew us a lot of smoke on Thanksgiving about the 'bee-keeper' veil look, remember? I may need to let him know that the dress is not totally bizarre."

"No, I'll tell him," Jenny responded. "Now that the dress is finished and obviously gorgeous, he has a right to know I won't be coming down the aisle in my cousin's debutante dress from ten years ago. Or in a red, feathered concoction. Actually, I should tell him now. He's at Mohr's, working, and he should be about ready for his dinner break."

"But we were going to dinner," Lauren said weakly.

"No, you and Bryan have some things to discuss," Jenny said with a grin. "I'll be out of here as soon as I can change."

"Well, 'fess up, Lauren," Bryan said after Jenny left. "How on earth did this all come about?"

"You know most of it, Bryan. Mavis was terrible to Jenny about the discount dress she'd picked, then Jenny cancelled the order, and then she was desperate to find a dress in time for the wedding." Lauren spoke in a rush, looking at the floor and wishing it would swallow her up.

"And your talent saved the day as Jenny said. It's a great dress and I know Bill will be blown away when he sees Jenny. And while I'm feeling courageous, this is why I thought your designs could work at Mohr's. I wasn't trying to use you. I wanted to come over so I could clear that up."

Lauren continued to look at the floor, hoping for a miracle disappearance. "I know that now, Bryan. I appreciate your evaluation of my design skills. I guess I should be honest and tell you I'm a little cautious about guys and their motives these days."

"Yeah, I'll bet you hear lots of bad things about men on your job."

Lauren thought about letting Bryan believe that was the only issue. But she knew it was time to be open with him, no matter what it cost her. With a combination of dread and hope, she responded. "It's not just that. Did you know I was engaged last year? And that we ended it?"

"Bill said something about that but I was in Europe on a buying trip the first part of the year. I didn't hear much about you and what's-his-name."

"Doug is his name. He's great until you disagree with him, want him to earn his keep, or don't buy into the concept of open marriage." Lauren paused. "I really sound bitter, huh?"

Bryan's face reddened slightly and his features were hard. "He's an idiot, Lauren," he said with grim determination. Then grinning, he added, "Want me beat him to a pulp?"

Lauren laughed in relief. At least he didn't think she was a total loser. Just that she had chosen one. "No need for rough stuff. I've hired that out for when he least expects it," she responded playfully. "Let's get some food. It's my treat this time, to celebrate the wedding dress being finished."

Lauren and Bryan chose Gordon's only cafeteria for their impromptu dinner. They were relaxed as they enjoyed the value plate specials. Feeling courageous, Lauren elaborated on her engagement to Doug.

"He's not a bad person," she said slowly. "Deep down he's very insecure and feels he has to prove himself to others. It's like he doesn't believe he can be himself and be accepted. I bought into a lot of it, at first. His flashy manner was so different from my introverted nature that I thought we were a good fit. There's some truth to opposites attracting but our values were so fundamentally opposed that the cracks in our relationship began to show pretty quickly."

Lauren stopped, blushing with humiliation. "Too much info, Bryan?"

Bryan's face showed his concern and continued anger at Doug. "It helps me know you better to hear this, Lauren. As I said, he's an idiot, a first class idiot."

They continued to eat in silence. Lauren regretted telling Bryan about her failure with Doug. What must he think of her now? He was so quiet. He probably couldn't wait to get away from her. She knew that any hope of a relationship with Bryan was over. He, obviously, couldn't get through the meal fast enough. Why would he want to spend time with someone who chose a man like that? And a woman who was a social worker, someone who should know the intricacies of human nature!

As they left the restaurant, Lauren noticed newly placed poinsettias in the lobby. Trying to fill the awkward silence between them, she said lightly, "I love the cream-colored poinsettias with pink tips. They're hard to find. One year my dad went all over the tri-county area looking for them to give to my mom." Bryan's silence confirmed her suspicion. She should never have told him about Doug.

Lauren went to church on Sunday morning for the first time in several months. She wondered how to reconcile her feelings for Bryan with the fear that still resided in her gut, the fear that she would be betrayed again, lied to, and ultimately left alone to pick up the pieces of her ego. As she prayed, she realized (again) that she should follow her own clinical advice: keep on working, doing her best, and giving the rest to God. She resolved to make this week a testament to God's forgiveness and constant chance for renewal.

After church, she spent the afternoon tidying her living room while listening to the Colts game in the background. She had decided before church to put a roast in the slow cooker and the house was now filled with the scent of beef, root vegetables, and a hint of garlic. She regretted that there was no one to share the food with. She'd be eating roast beef sandwiches for the next two weeks.

There was a knock on the door and Lauren thought hopefully that Bryan might have stopped by again. She was disappointed, however. Shocked was actually a better word than disappointed. Totally surprised, caught off-guard, and vulnerable. Just the way Doug wanted.

"Hey, Sunshine, you look great!" Doug bellowed as he made his way into the living room. "I can't get over what you've done with this little place and how good it smells in here."

As always, Doug looked perfectly put together. His dark hair was combed straight back with just enough hair product to help it stay put. He was dressed in cream slacks and a lightweight blue sweater, sans coat. Inappropriate attire for early December in Indiana but, somehow, he made it work.

"What do you want, Doug?" Lauren whispered. "I thought you moved to Louisville for that new job." Lauren reeled from the unexpected intrusion into her peaceful Sunday. Giving it to God had not included a visit from Doug.

"Honey, that's no welcome for the man you were going to marry, is it? I'm in town to see some friends and I wanted to touch base with you, of course."

"Funny, you don't have any friends here that I know of," Lauren said snidely. "And why would I want to touch base with you?"

"Lauren, you never had much of a sense of humor, did you? Fact is, I'm relocating to Indianapolis and, since it's so close, I wanted to see you. I've thought a lot about what happened with us and I think we should both honor all the good things we had and give it another try."

Every fiber in Lauren's being wished that she had her carving knife, which was in the kitchen, fortunately. It would be satisfying to make Doug feel off balance for a change. She had a sudden flash of awareness and empathy for impulsive clients who later regretted threatening others in anger. But she forced herself to stay calm and was able to smile at Doug while she responded to his ridiculous plan.

"'Honor all the good things we had?'" Lauren said, her voice steely. "Help me understand, Doug. I remember a flawed diamond engagement ring, a ring that was the perfect symbol of our relationship. A relationship flawed in most ways as a matter of fact, missing communication, respect, and fidelity. And I'm willing to own that I was a part of that, Doug. I let too many things slide because I wanted to get married so badly. So you did me a favor by sleeping with your boss. You gave the me out I needed."

As she spoke, Lauren had clarity she'd been seeking for months. It wasn't just Doug's fault. She had been willing to overlook too much. No man was perfect but she couldn't deal with lies or being mocked. Thank the heavens above they hadn't married or, even worse, had children.

Doug was not deterred; in fact, he seemed to relish Lauren's opposition. He'd always liked a good fight and he performed better under pressure than Lauren did. "Honey, you're taking on too much responsibility. It was me, all me. I've been seeing a great counselor. You'd really like her. She's helped me see that I was selfish from the start. Every penny I've spent on those sessions has been worth gold. I've changed so much. And it's time I showed you that. Before you find someone else."

Lauren was appalled that Doug had been seeing a counselor. Not because she didn't believe in the effectiveness of psychotherapy but because he had adamantly refused to see a therapist in the past. While they were together, hanging on despite their constant arguments after he was caught with his boss, she had begged him to go to couples counseling. He had ridiculed her suggestion, saying only losers would tell a stranger about their private troubles.

She tried to keep her response light but without success. "I'm glad therapy has helped you, Doug. Hope you and your therapist haven't gotten too close during all the discussions of our relationship."

"There you go, Lauren. Just when I'm trying to make a new start and show you I've changed, you bring up my past mistakes. And just after you admitted that you were a part of our problems."

Lauren sighed. "You're right, Doug. Our problems were related to both of us. But that doesn't mean it's good to start over. I've moved on and so have you most likely."

Despite herself, she was curious about his life. "What's with the new job in Indy?"

Doug seemed to sense a partial victory in Lauren's question. "Well, after my idiot boss in Louisville made unrealistic sales goals for the team, I decided Indiana suited me better. I'm part of a start-up that deals in direct marketing with coupons targeted to women."

"Start-up? That usually involves heavy investment, doesn't it?" Lauren's skepticism was obvious. Doug never had money in savings, insisting that when he hit it big the windfall would be his financial safety net.

"Well, it's not a start-up per se. It's a franchise and I was able to get a loan on great terms," Doug said proudly.

"Good for you, Doug." Lauren was doubtful the loan was made on great terms but at least Doug was still working at something. His job record had been spotty at best, especially since he lost his post after sleeping with his manager. Maybe owning a franchise would improve his work ethic.

"So, we should celebrate my return and my new job," Doug said. "Do I smell your award-winning pot roast? Can't an old friend stay for Sunday dinner?"

Lauren waffled. It would be rude to send him away since he knew the food was ready. "Okay, let's eat. But I have a full evening after dinner, so you'll have to be on your way."

"I understand, Lauren. I remember how your Sunday evenings were busy reviewing case notes for the coming week. But I really appreciate the chance to catch up and enjoy some great cooking." As usual, Doug made himself at home in Lauren's dining room, setting the table for two, using her good china.

Despite herself, Lauren had a good time sharing her dinner with Doug. He seemed less egocentric than in the past, asking genuine questions about her job and Jenny's upcoming wedding. She surprised herself by telling the story of the wedding gown and how it had helped her get past her lonely depression.

"I'm sorry you've been down, baby, and I admit

I'm a part of that. You have to believe I would never be unfaithful again. It's not who I am anymore."

Lauren was about to tell Doug not to call her "baby" when the doorbell rang. Since Doug was ready to launch his rationale about why he was a new man and worthy of a second chance, she welcomed the interruption. She was shocked to see Bryan at the door with two creamy, pink-tipped poinsettia plants. In contrast to Doug's sophisticated outfit, Bryan was dressed for the weather, wearing a black parka over faded jeans. Lined hiking boots completed his look.

"Uh, I thought I'd come by with these after you told me how much you liked them at dinner last night. But I see you're busy," Bryan said, peering past Lauren to see who was at her dining room table.

Exploding inwardly but maintaining her composure, Lauren smiled stiffly. "Bryan, this is Doug Mathas. Doug, meet Bryan Dawson," she said weakly.

Doug's response was smooth. He acted genuinely pleased to meet Bryan. "Hey there, Bryan. Lauren didn't tell me she was seeing anyone else. She and I have quite a history and we were just catching up over her great cooking."

Bryan was equally pleasant. "Lauren and I are in my cousin's wedding on New Year's Day, so we've been thrown together a lot lately."

Thrown together? Evidently, Bryan didn't think their dinner last night, complete with her revealing the pain Doug had caused her, meant anything more than filling his stomach.

Both men faked a chuckle and Bryan said his

good-byes. After Bryan was out of earshot, Lauren looked at Doug with daggers.

"Could you have been more misleading? You implied we were getting back together!"

"So I do have some competition," Doug said smugly. "Believe me, Lauren, we have something real between us and I'm not going to let Bryan ruin it."

"We have nothing between us, Doug. It's time for you to leave."

After Doug exited with a confident smile, the house was quiet. Lauren looked at the dirty dishes and half-eaten roast. So much for giving it to God. How was she going to deal with this mess? And she wasn't referring to her kitchen and dining room.

Bryan was livid. What was Lauren doing with the man she referred to with pain in her eyes each time she mentioned his name? They seemed very cozy; he had heard them talking quietly, almost intimately, as he approached Lauren's door. Her description of Doug's cheating must have been a lie because he could never imagine her chatting with a man who betrayed her that way. And her subsequent depression must have been proof that she wasn't over him, despite her protests to the contrary.

Well, it was good that he knew before he really fell for her. She wasn't the stable, grounded woman she appeared to be. Bryan had a sudden memory flash of a fight his parents had when he was around twelve. Tom was angry about Sally's friendship with a banker in town. At the time Bryan thought they would divorce but within a few weeks, the atmosphere at home was calm again. Not that his parents were ever close but they seemed to go back to their pattern of living separate, but amicable, lives.

Was there really such a thing as a happy marriage? His brother Jeff, and his wife Mandy, seemed to be good together but they lived too far away to know for certain. Even Lauren's parents had a lot of trouble when her dad was laid off. That line of thinking eventually led Bryan to turn on the Colts game and have a supper of microwaved popcorn while half reclining on the couch.

"Doug Mathas sure had a better meal than this," he said aloud to the television.

Chapter Seven

Lauren was busy at work even before her shift started. She was reviewing charts when her administrative assistant knocked on her door. "Lauren, there's a guy on the phone who says he has to speak with you immediately but I'm not sure if you want to talk to him," Shirley said. "It's Doug Mathas. He's very persistent."

Lauren sighed. Doug was following his usual pattern. He would catch her when she was focused on work and mount a full onslaught of charm until she gave in. But this time she wouldn't give in.

"It's okay. I'll take it, Shirley," she said. After Doug clicked on, she asked politely, "What's got you up this early on a Monday, Doug? It's unusual for you to be awake at eight."

"Lauren, it's not like you to be mean," he said. "I wanted to see if you were busy this evening. I'd love to repay you for that excellent dinner last night."

"Not available tonight, tomorrow night, or ever, Doug. I'm glad things are going so well for you and that you've been helped by your work in therapy.

But I thought a lot about our history after you left and I'm at peace. There's really no point in trying to resurrect what we had which wasn't all that much when you look at the big picture."

"You're not thinking clearly, I can tell." Doug said with a combination of charm and concern. "It's Dawson, isn't it? Just because he's the heir to a big business fortune doesn't mean he's the perfect man for you."

"Could you be more insulting, Doug? As if I'd be involved with someone just for his money? Surely you should know that's not the case, given your constant shortage of funds. You even asked my parents for a loan right before we broke up!" Lauren was hot with rage and her phone alert light was on, indicating that her first client had arrived. "I've got to go now, Doug. Don't call me again," she ordered.

Lauren took five minutes to compose herself before she greeted Penny, her first client of the day. Penny was fifteen, grieving the divorce of her parents and unhappy at her new school, to which she had been moved by her mother after the split.

"How has your week been, Penny?" Lauren asked. Penny then launched into a venting, weeping, and anxiety-ridden rant about the details of her many challenges in the last few days. Lauren was able to engage with the pretty young girl and thoughts of Doug and Bryan disappeared for the rest of the session. She and Penny did productive work as Lauren encouraged her to feel her sadness while not getting lost in hopelessness that things would never get better. She tried to explore the possible reasons for Penny's parents' divorce but Penny remained obstinate, insisting her mother was the only partner at fault. As she had in their prior meetings, Lauren asked Penny if her mother might attend a few sessions and, as before, Penny refused.

"Nope, she's not coming here," Penny said firmly. "This is my time and she's not allowed in."

Lauren caught the implicit punishment Penny was inflicting on her mother but let it pass for now. "Fine, it's your call," she said. "But I think eventually it would help you understand each other better to be in the same room when you talk about all the things you're dealing with."

The day flowed smoothly for a Monday. Lauren was not covering triage, so she was able to do chart notes and return phone calls during her lunch hour. After trying unsuccessfully to chew the dry roast beef sandwich she'd packed in her lunch bag, she made do with yogurt. She smiled to herself as she blamed Doug for ruining her week of leftovers.

Lauren then laughed out loud at her silliness and at her inability to admit that her own choices had led to the dinner with Doug. She guessed this was progress. She told him not to call and she could laugh because the roast tasted like leather. Maybe giving it to God was helping. She gave a silent prayer of thanks and returned to her desk.

As she drove home later, she thought about calling Bryan to explain the situation he had walked in on the night before. Surely he would understand that Doug had come over without an invitation and good manners had been the reason he stayed for supper. Or not. What would she think if the situation were reversed? She would feel betrayed. Her chest tightened as she realized she had hurt Bryan. He was a good man and deserved better.

Despite these troubling thoughts, Lauren decided she wasn't up to a phone call to Bryan. Her feelings were too muddled to handle an apology and his probable reaction. Without Jenny's dress to work on, her evening seemed never-ending. Television, even her beloved HGTV, felt stale. She had to think of a new project or she was going to turn into a cat lady.

As she sipped some tea, she had an idea. Jenny's dress had evolved in part from her creating costumes and other outfits for children in the community. What if she offered a service, via the food pantry, to parents who couldn't afford the latest in costumes or party dresses? Could she manage this new responsibility and still stay fresh for her job?

Sure I could. I have to fill these lonely evenings or I'll sink back into the blues. And, obviously, Bryan Dawson isn't going to be around.

Lauren phoned the director of the food pantry. They brainstormed a process to offer one item of handmade clothing each week to pantry participants. Her next call was to Jenny.

Jenny listened quietly as Lauren filled her in on the new plan to keep herself busy while helping others. Lauren detailed Doug's unexpected appearance and Bryan's frosty reaction.

Jenny was skeptical about Lauren's plan to sew for the food pantry clients but avoided commentary on Doug. "One outfit each week is pretty ambitious, Lauren. You told me you couldn't handle making my flower girl's dress when I joked about that. What if you have plans, a date or two, or you need to be available to your parents?" Jenny deliberately avoided Bryan's name but Lauren knew what she meant.

"It will be fine, Jenny. I can knock out a child's dress in an evening. I'll restrict the patterns to those I've sewn before with simple lines and minimal decoration."

"Hmm…. Not exactly the type of outfit kids want these days, do you think? Have you been to Mohr's lately to see what kind of clothing is on trend for little girls? They're not selling royal family traditional, you know. More like a combo of Beyoncé and Taylor Swift. You forget that I was easy with my wedding gown. I wanted simple lines but girls today may not."

Lauren was concerned. Jenny had a good point. Her need to occupy her evenings while feeling like a savior was clouding her judgment about what would actually serve her food pantry clients.

"And another thing," Jenny continued, filling the lull in the conversation. "Have you forgotten that my wedding is just a few weeks away? You have serious maid of honor responsibilities waiting for you."

"Yes, I've been avoiding those as well. I've got to plan a bachelorette party. Should I be booking a Chippendale?" Lauren teased, knowing that Jenny would never consider such a thing.

"No need for that. I was thinking that we could all go to the spa on the river and have a girls' weekend there. The salon is very good. The food is fantastic for the price, despite the lack of calories." Jenny paused. "Lauren, I know this is tough for you, what with Doug's reappearance and the uncertainty with Bryan. The other girls could fill in with all the bachelorette planning."

Lauren blinked back tears. Jenny was such a kind person. "No, absolutely not. I want to do this. We've been besties since grade school, Jenny! Who else would be able to both honor and embarrass you at the same time?"

Jenny laughed. Lauren was relieved. The idea of planning a bachelorette party was comforting because her evenings now had purpose. The adoption of a stray cat could wait a little longer.

After seeing Doug at Lauren's, Bryan worked on autopilot for the next few days. He couldn't get the image of them having a cozy dinner out of his head. Doug was a looker, for sure. His Mediterranean heritage served him well, providing olive skin and thick, dark hair. Worse than that, however, was Doug's confident swagger and knowledge that he had caught Bryan by surprise. Bryan hated not being in control and this experience was the epitome of that feeling. Well, Lauren had made her choice. Obviously, she was happier with Doug than she let on, despite him hooking up with his boss.

Once again Bryan was shocked at Lauren's ability to overlook such a betrayal. Maybe she was intent on rewriting the story of her relationship with Doug. Some women were like that. Or maybe she was like him and hated to fail. Great. He and Lauren were both into control and being successful, no matter what. Not the best ingredients for a healthy relationship. They'd drive each other nuts.

Lauren had also thrown herself into work during the week following the "Pot Roast Fiasco," as she was calling it. She wondered about Bryan's silence. Before he saw her with Doug, they had been talking almost every day. Surely he didn't think anything was going on with her and Doug? She was realistic, though, as she remembered Bryan's shocked expression and Doug's confident air as she introduced them to each other. Bryan was hurt, no doubt about it. She just didn't want to admit she'd ruined things between them. Perhaps she could make it better, somehow.

After talking to Jenny about the bachelorette party, she decided to call Bryan after work on Friday. Enough was enough. They were grown-ups and they should be able to talk this through.

Despite her good intentions, nothing resulted from her calls. Each of her three attempts to reach Bryan went directly to voice mail, with no return call all night.

As she usually did when she was frustrated, Lauren responded with activity. Her bedroom closet was jammed with clothing from grad school and beyond. She emptied the racks, throwing the hangers filled with a jumble of styles and colors onto her bed. Laughing, she tried on dated slacks, interview suits with heavily padded shoulders, and an assortment of sweaters in garish colors.

As she looked at the pile of discards, she tallied a list for donation to the local thrift store. Her fortunate life stared back at her via the stack of perfectly good clothes headed for charity. How could she be such a baby? She had so much to be grateful for. Culling her possessions was good for the soul and culling the men in her life was also a worthy endeavor. Too bad she was the one being culled by a certain Bryan Dawson.

The next day, Lauren went to the food pantry. She spoke to the director about putting her "one dress a week" plan on hold, given all her commitments to Jenny's bachelorette weekend and wedding. As she had expected, the pantry was busier than usual since the holidays were approaching fast. Sign-ups for Christmas gifts from Santa were also being held. Parents could request one gift per child, to be wrapped and labeled by volunteers.

"I'd forgotten how the rhythm changes in early December," Lauren told Jenny. "I sure hope the volunteers for Santa's gifts are better than last year. Remember how we ended up doing most of the wrapping on the Friday night before pick-up?"

Jenny almost shouted in response. "Do I remember? You bet! The only things that got us through were multiple espressos and the thought of the kids' faces when they opened the gifts. What brought it home for me, though, was hearing from the kids in January. Several of them said their pantry gift was the only one under the tree."

"Have you heard from Bryan?" Jenny continued. "You haven't mentioned him all week."

"Let's talk when we eat," Lauren replied stiffly.

After the auditorium had been cleared and swept, Lauren and Jenny decided that they deserved serious holiday comfort food for their efforts. They were settled in at the local cafeteria, both having chosen turkey and dressing.

"Thanksgiving, part two," Jenny joked. "So what gives with Bryan?"

"Good question. He's not answering my calls. When he saw Doug at my place, he was angry. We had brief introductions and he left in a hurry."

"What exactly were you and Doug doing?" Jenny said, catching her breath and obviously dreading what she might hear from her best friend.

"Eating the roast I'd made. Talking about Doug's new job and his reformed character. No big deal," Lauren noted defensively.

"Um, it's probably a big deal in Bryan's eyes. Have you ever cooked for Bryan?"

"There's never been an opportunity, Jenny," Lauren said. "I've paid for dinner once. And I didn't cook for Doug either! He just dropped in and smelled the roast. It would have been rude to ignore that it was time for Sunday supper."

"Lauren, you should keep trying to call Bryan," Jenny ordered. "I don't blame him for feeling hurt, angry, or whatever. And maybe you should ask yourself why you rolled out the welcome mat for a guy who treated you like dirt. If you had a client who'd welcomed her ex for an impromptu supper, you'd be confronting her, right?"

Lauren's cheeks reddened. She felt like her best friend had slapped her. She looked at Jenny with surprise but knew Jenny didn't have an unkind bone in her body.

"I guess I'll do some thinking about my motives, Jenny. But you really can't believe I'd give Doug another chance, can you?"

"I hope not, Lauren. But I'm worried about you. My prayer list just got one item longer."

Trying to ease the tension between them, Jenny changed topics by discussing her shopping trip for toys for the children at the food pantry. "Boy, I didn't realize how much video games cost," she puffed. "When Bill and I have children, they'll be playing with blocks and dolls. No tech gifts allowed."

"Good luck with that," Lauren said. "I agree with your sentiment but it's probably not workable with today's kids."

"Yeah, I know. But my kids will play outside each day and TV will be limited." Jenny's brow wrinkled as she spoke.

"What's up now, Jenny? You look really concerned. Is Mavis stocking up on tech toys for future little Sturms?"

"No, it's not her, for a change. We're getting closer if you can believe it. After the bridal shower, she asked if Bill and I were going to start a family soon."

"Wow, what did you say?" Lauren asked.

"I said I'd love kids right away but that it would depend on lots of factors. What surprised me was that Mavis said she was supportive of anything we wanted to do, except naming a little girl after her, since she's always hated her name. Evidently, it's a family tradition to name the first girl after great-great-great-grandma Mavis Whoever. Sally was born a year after Mavis and got a normal name."

"I'm glad to hear that," Lauren said. "Not about Mavis hating her name but about you two bonding. If she raised Bill, she has to have some redeeming qualities, right?"

"Right. Mavis is a good mom but too invested in putting on a show for the community. And her rivalry with Sally is silly. I can't believe they're still as close as they are."

Jenny continued. "Changing subjects again, when I was buying toys for the pantry kids it hit me how early kids today get sucked into wanting more and more of everything. You wouldn't believe how many tantrums I witnessed and how many parents gave in just to keep the peace."

Lauren nodded. "Relationships and parenting are hard," she said. "I see it in my clients at work and at the food pantry. Maybe getting married just isn't in my future. You and Bill are a natural fit. You'll be good partners and good parents. I'm not sure if there's anyone like that out there for me."

"Oh, stop it," Jenny scoffed. "I won't let you whine on like this. Yes, Doug was a bad fit for you. Maybe he'll settle down with someone else but you gave him loads of chances and it's over. There's someone better for you, I know it."

"You sound like my mother," Lauren groaned. "Better watch yourself."

Chapter Eight

Work brought its usual challenges that week. Penny's appearance at her appointment was startling. The formerly well-groomed, tidy teen was now sporting purple hair and a small wrist tattoo of a spider.

Lauren was careful not to show her shock. "I'd ask how things are going, Penny but I see you've been busy. Let's start with the hair. What gives?"

"I decided it was time to wake my mom up," Penny retorted. "She's so in love with the latest loser that she needed something to get her mind off of him. Before you ask, the tattoo is temporary but she doesn't know that. She's so mad at me she can't see straight. She even threatened to take me out of counseling as if these behaviors, as she calls them, are the result of our meetings!" Penny was full of drama as she air-quoted the word behavior.

Lauren tried to tread carefully. "So your mom's with a loser and evidently you're worried because he's not the first one since the divorce. You certainly have provided her with powerful distractions!

Other than threatening to take you out of therapy, how did she react? Did you tell your mom about how scared you are for her?"

"She reacted by grounding me for two weeks," Penny said. "No, I didn't talk to her about the latest and greatest boyfriend because it wouldn't have done any good. Anything I say about him will cause more fights between us."

"Remember when I suggested that she come in with you for a session or two? This might be the right time to do that. We wouldn't have to focus on you, just on your concerns about your mom's friend. Also, I have to ask. Penny, have these losers done anything to you?"

"No, I knew you'd ask though," Penny said with a groan. "They're not creepy, just unemployed, late on their child support, and full of themselves."

"Right. Then let's talk tattoos," Lauren said conversationally. "I have a friend who runs a successful shop in Indy and she says you should think hard about getting a permanent tattoo immediately after a tough time in your life. So I'm glad yours is temporary."

"Why not?" Penny asked. "I think that if you get something visible to remind you that you were a survivor when everything was going wrong, it would be a good thing."

"It would also remind you of that particular time, wouldn't it?" Lauren asked. "Think about it. So many folks get a tattoo right after a death, divorce, break up, or job loss. If it were me, it would be hard to let go of a time that made me sad if I saw a tattoo every day – when I brushed my teeth, checked the time, cooked dinner, all that."

"Well, I'm not an oldster, like you, so I don't wear a watch to check the time. My phone is my clock," Penny scoffed. "I'm still thinking about something permanent, so give it up, Lauren."

"You're right. Enough for now," Lauren said mildly. "But when you want something permanent, be sure you get someone who does good work. It's expensive but worth it. You don't want a tat that looks like a first-grader went to town on your arm."

Penny grunted in response, so Lauren decided sufficient time had been spent on the pros and cons of body ink. Lauren was sure that Penny would tell her mother she was in favor of a large, full-arm sleeve if she kept pushing.

"Where'd you get the idea for your hair?" Lauren asked.

"Oh, from a friend. All the east coast girls in the fashion magazines have intense color on their hair." Penny's eyes focused on the ceiling as she replied.

"What's his name?" Lauren wondered, also looking at the office's popcorn ceiling.

"Great, Lauren. You immediately assumed a guy influenced me to color my hair. I'm not that needy."

Lauren gave in. "So, what else?" she asked.

"Same ole, same ole," Penny chirped.

Lauren waited patiently.

"In addition to her fit about the hair and tattoo, Mom's her usual drudge self. According to her, my room is a health hazard."

"Well, is it? Describe your room to me," Lauren said.

Penny arched her brow. "What was your room like when you were fifteen? You describe your room first."

"How would that help you, Penny?"

"Lame therapist answer," Penny grunted.

Lauren laughed. "Okay, you win this one. My room was tiny because each of my parents used the larger bedrooms for their offices. So I had stuff piled everywhere with a ten-inch path from the door to my bed."

Actually, Dad's office was also his man-cave for drinking when he was between jobs. Thank the Lord that didn't last long.

"Your parents screwed you out of a decent room?" Penny squealed. "That's awful. Did your years of therapy pay off? I'll bet you have a HUGE room now to make up for it. Isn't that called compensating for your past angst?"

Lauren smiled, pleased with Penny's hostility. Something was about to shift in Penny's attitude toward counseling.

Penny kept on. "Seriously, what's your room like now?"

"My room is cozy and it's a reflection of my personality. That's how rooms are, Penny. Whether you like it or not, your space reflects who you are, what's happening in your life, how you look at the world." Lauren knew that continued discussion of Penny's room would be pointless. "But let's get back to talking about your mom."

"Mom's not been that bad, actually," Penny said. "But she won't let me hang with my friends without the third degree. And this new loser backs her up. As if it's any of his business."

Lauren paused again, letting silence fill the room.

"Maybe it is time for Mom to come in with me,"

Penny said softly. "But I don't want you to take her side!"

Lauren responded softly, matching Penny's tone. "Whether you believe it or not, I'll be taking whatever side I think is in your best interest, Penny."

"Another lame therapist response," Penny drawled. "Anyway, time's up for today, as you always say." Lauren noticed, though, that as she made her next appointment, Penny was clear with the scheduler that her mother would also be attending.

Lauren felt better. It was time to see the real dynamic between Penny and her mother. Lauren's experience told her Penny's mom was not as clueless as Penny thought and that Penny was still intent on her parents' reconciling. It was almost every kid's fantasy after their parents split. But it didn't usually happen.

Due to the upcoming holidays, food pantry volunteers met midweek to wrap Christmas gifts. A new set of volunteers assembled to help, including members of the Women's Hospital Auxiliary. Each member introduced herself and one attractive, well-dressed woman greeted Jenny with a hug. Jenny introduced her as "Bill's aunt, Sally Dawson."

Lauren had met Sally years ago. The older woman was always complimentary of Lauren's high school sewing awards. Lauren was again struck by Sally's beauty and by Bryan's resemblance to his mother.

"Hello, Lauren," Sally said graciously. "I've heard from Bryan that you have a lovely home and a demanding job at the mental health center. How are your parents?"

"They're good, Sally. Thanks for your kind words about my house. It's still very unfinished but I enjoy a project."

Volunteers were paired with pantry regulars for wrapping duties. Lauren and Sally ended up as partners. To Lauren's surprise, Sally was chatty throughout their shift. She discussed her charity work, her feeling of distance from her husband, and her sadness that Bryan hadn't found anyone to settle down with. Lauren was initially sympathetic to Sally's feelings but her radar went active when Sally spoke of Bryan's lack of a life partner. Was Sally fishing for information or unaware she and Bryan weren't speaking? Was she hinting that Lauren was not in their league and to step away from her son?

Lauren responded to Sally's openness with practiced noncommittal statements, trying to ignore her own paranoia. She focused on Sally, not her son, and sympathized with Sally's feelings of loneliness.

"They say we live in a lonely time," Lauren said. "It's hard for people to connect when there's Facebook, Instagram, and Twitter available to 'talk' without having to be face-to-face with the person you want to know. And the nuances that personal conversations provide are lost in social media messages."

"Yes, it was simpler in my time. Not that I'm old or anything!" Sally laughed. "But we all grew up together in a small town and knew each other's families and friends. Bryan says that's not such a great thing, though. I sometimes wonder if he feels he owes his dad and me his service to the store.

Maybe he wants to leave Gordon for a bigger city."

"I've never heard him say that but such a big business organization has to be burdensome for all of you," Lauren replied.

"It wasn't in the past but now, with all the competition, it's more difficult," Sally said, pursing her lips. "The larger chain stores sell everything we do and they can be more competitive on pricing. Even our friend Stan, who owns Bailey's Jewelry, is struggling. He says everybody sells fine jewelry these days, even Walmart!"

Lauren laughed and agreed. They were finished with their wrapping chores and Lauren thanked Sally for her help.

"No problem, Lauren," Sally replied. "I've enjoyed this more than any other volunteer project this year. Maybe we could meet sometime for lunch and you could tell me more about the Food Pantry."

"Sounds good, Sally. We're always looking for helpers. There are lots of positions to be filled each week."

At home later, Sally reflected on the pleasant time she'd had wrapping Christmas gifts for the food pantry clients. The task seemed more meaningful, more real, to her than the countless charity lunches, which tended to focus on the most efficient (sometimes gimmicky) way to raise money for a cause. The food pantry work was hard, (her back was killing her after several hours of measuring and cutting gift wrap), but the task had a satisfying begin-and-end quality that traditional fundraising lacked.

The other surprise was the engaging time she had with Lauren. Sally remembered Bryan mentioning her a few times but, lately, he had been so moody she hadn't asked any questions. Lauren hadn't discussed Bryan much either but she was passionate as she spoke about her work at the mental health center. Sally's eyes misted as she remembered her own previous passion, teaching first grade, but that had ended when she married. Tom had been firm about Sally devoting her time to the community, both to share their blessings and to enhance the image of Mohr's brand. Soon after, the boys were born in quick succession and Sally was overwhelmed with parenting and the charity commitments she had made.

Not that she had minded all that much. Tom was rarely home and, even then, he was distracted by work. And he was always pressuring the boys in whatever sport they were playing that season. If she hadn't built a life of ladies' lunches and committees, she'd have lost her mind.

That thought led Sally to review the current state of her marriage. She loved Tom with all of her being but, despite repeated questioning, he wouldn't share his current tension with her. He had always worried about the business but this time was different. He was more serious but less energized. And, unlike the past, he wasn't pushing her to enhance the brand by purchasing the latest personal and home fashions.

Things, obviously, weren't going well at Mohr's. When business was good, Tom had demanded they build their huge house but now he complained about her extravagance! She had to figure out how to help him but he wouldn't talk to her. Maybe Bryan knew what was going on. She resolved to ask the next time she saw him.

Sally was a pragmatist, however. She knew she needed to take care of herself. Spending more time at the food pantry would do her a lot of good. She already had several ideas to increase their funding.

Never one to ignore an impulse, Sally found the pantry phone number, connecting with the director, who hadn't yet left the pantry site. Once she mentioned Lauren's name (whom she discovered held the title of Volunteer Coordinator), Sally was booked for immediate training.

"Good," she said to Izzy, her attentive Yorkie. "Time for a new challenge and also time to count my blessings. I've been getting a little morose lately."

Saturday arrived and Sally checked in with the director. Lauren walked up and smiled. "Sally, you said you might join us in the future but I didn't think it would happen until after the holidays. Instead, you're already trained and ready to go!"

"I'm all set, Lauren. And I'll bet an extra hand this week will be helpful!"

"Absolutely," Lauren agreed. "Since Christmas is almost here, today we're distributing small hams and canned sweet potatoes, in addition to the usual staples. Then we're open Wednesday evening and we'll be adding corned beef briskets and cabbage to the usual offerings. Do you think you can come then too?"

"Love to," Sally answered. "My holiday preparations are pretty much finished, so the pantry will be a great way to feel the spirit of the season."

At the end of the day, Sally wondered about her initial enthusiasm. "My trainer, Misty, has never driven me this hard," Sally chuckled as she said goodbye to Lauren. "Talk about an upper body workout! Lifting those hams and canned goods was brutal!" She cringed at the thought of Wednesday's briskets and heads of cabbage. "I'll know to take some pain relievers before I come next time!"

As she drove home, Sally focused on the future of the pantry, given the sparse stockroom she had noticed at each of her shifts. Some restocking had been done but the shelves were emptier than the first time she'd volunteered. Without some additional funding, they'd be handing out bread and peanut butter in a few months. Her money-raising instincts kicked in and she had a pleasant evening planning ways to make the pantry more sustainable in the future.

"What's got you so revved up?" Tom asked after dinner. "You barely spoke while we ate. Is anything wrong?"

"No, not at all. I spent the day at the food pantry and I loved it. They do lots of good work. I'm going back Wednesday. Their funds are always iffy, though. I've been thinking about how to help in that area too."

Tom looked at his wife closely. "Sally, I haven't seen you this happy in a while," he commented. "But what about your other charities? You don't want to let them down."

"Not to worry, Tom. They practically run themselves at this point and, to be honest, some of the younger volunteers have much better ideas for fundraising than I do. Can you believe next year's event for the children's hospital is for each contributing organization to decorate a patient room? My sorority's new members came up with that idea. Our suite will be done in nautical décor to go with our founders' theme."

Sally paused and took the risk to ask Tom about Mohr's. "So what's new with you and the store, Tom?" She held her breath, expecting to be put off again by her husband.

"What's new? Not much unfortunately and that's our problem. But I don't want you to worry, Sally. Just focus on the pantry."

"Don't patronize me, Tom Dawson," she replied, as she slapped the elegant maple dining table. "I'm your wife and I know Mohr's isn't doing well. Let me in on things. We always used to solve problems together."

Tom was both shocked and pleased by his wife's outburst. "I thought you didn't care about the business, Sally."

"I care about you, Tom. I read and watch the news. I know independent retailers in all areas, like clothing, restaurants, and pharmacies, are struggling. And in a tiny market like Gordon, we have a limited customer base to draw on."

Tom laughed, but his eyes were serious. "You nailed it, Sally. You just summarized in a few sentences what it took three consultants six months to say."

Sally fixed her gaze on her husband. "What's the plan, Tom? Is Mohr's going to downsize, close, be solely an on-line retailer? What did those consultants recommend?"

"Good grief, sweetheart, you could have saved me a lot of money if we'd had this conversation in March. Those are the exact options they included in their final report. Their primary recommendations were the most obvious: close the store and establish an on-line presence if we desire. They were all consummate bean counters with no experience serving customers. Meeting customers' needs, establishing personal relationships in a small community, none of that mattered to them. And I doubt if their combined ages totaled more than seventy-five years. I swear, one kid still smelled like his mom's basement!"

"Bryan and I are stuck, though," Tom continued. "I guess we're waiting for some kind of marketing miracle to save Mohr's."

Sally switched from problem-solving to loving-wife mode. "I know none of those solutions feel good, Tom. You and Bryan are brilliant men and you'll figure out the best ways to deal with Mohr's. What I want to you to know, though, is that I'll be on board with whatever you decide. We have plenty for our needs, our retirements are funded, and we've got independent, self-sufficient sons. I could downsize from this mansion in a heartbeat!" she said, only half teasing.

Tom smiled in relief. "I love you, Sally. I've lost touch with how we used to be together. Fighting the odds, building the business, working as a team."

"That's still us, Tom," Sally said softly. "I miss the closeness of those times too."

Chapter Nine

After her latest interaction with Sally, Lauren dismissed her worries about not being good enough for Bryan. She called his cell and he picked up on the second ring.

"Hi there," she said. "I wanted to follow up because we haven't talked since you stopped by. Doug was just leaving when you came in. There was no need for you to take off. Or to ignore my many calls since then!"

"Really? Doug was just leaving? You two looked pretty cozy to me," Bryan said stiffly. "And he got home cooking!"

Lauren chuckled at his funny, pouty voice. "You're right. I've never cooked for you. How about if we fix that. Could you come for dinner on Saturday? We can also talk about what you think you walked in on last Sunday. Are there any foods you can't or won't eat?"

Bryan said he'd eat anything but spicy Thai food, which was not an issue since Lauren didn't like it either. She ended the call feeling relieved

Bryan had accepted her invitation. Neither of them mentioned Sally. Lauren realized Bryan had probably not spoken to his mother about her work at the pantry. It was just as well. She had to reassure Bryan that Doug was not back in her life. No sense muddying the waters with a discussion of his mother's concerns. She wanted Bryan to know he was important to her. It scared her but not letting him know about her feelings was even scarier.

Lauren went to work on Monday with a better attitude than she'd had in weeks. She was almost finished with her chart notes when her supervisor, Dr. Cheaney, asked to see her.

"Lauren, I've been meaning to talk to you for a few days but the changes at corporate weren't finalized until late Friday afternoon," he opened. "They're closing some of the smaller clinics in the seven-county area, which means we'll be absorbing clients and staff from the other offices."

Lauren tensed, wondering if she'd be out of a job soon. Corporate changes had never been good for her father, always resulting in him being laid off. Would absorbing staff from other offices result in her losing her position?

Dr. Cheaney continued. "It's a unanimous choice that you should run this office, Lauren. You have good clinical skills combined with insightful gut reactions to clients. I'll be in the main building starting the first of the year, acting as supervisor for all eight remaining clinics, so we'll connect monthly in person and as needed for phone consultations."

Shocked, Lauren paused, then answered. "Can I have a little time to consider this, Dr. Cheaney? What are the expectations for work hours? I'm here for nine hours most days and I don't want to get stale. I also have volunteer work that's important to me and I need energy for that."

"Understood, Lauren," he replied. "That's one of the qualities the C-suite agreed would make you a good fit for the clinic director position. You have the ability to compartmentalize just enough, so you don't get burned out with all the demands mental health work entails. You would rotate on-call duties with the other clinic directors, so you would actually take less call than you do now. And of course, the director position has a higher pay scale."

I've been hiding my burnout better than I realized, Lauren thought. Jenny's wedding has helped with that. Bryan has too, I guess.

The meeting ended with the agreement that Lauren would give Dr. Cheaney her answer after the first of the year. She had a lot to think about. The increase in salary would be helpful but what would the tradeoffs be? She had enough money to make ends meet now, especially since she'd finally paid off her grad school loans.

Lauren's introspective nature kicked into high gear as she walked back to her office. Her graduate program director had frequently admonished her cohort about the importance of representing their university.

"You are graduating from one of the premier MSW programs in the country," he would lecture. "If you think a job as a run-of-the-mill social worker is career success, you are mistaken. This college of social work churns out directors, national professional association officers, and members of every state board. I expect that each of you will honor this tradition by excelling in this most noble of professions."

Lauren stewed as she recalled his words but she smiled at the joke she and the other students had shared about him. He could pontificate about a grocery list if asked.

Wasn't working hard, and ethically, for your clients enough anymore? Was she a disgrace to her college if that was enough for her? How was a high-quality professional supposed to balance all of those other roles – clinic director, board member, national officer? And what about having a family, or connecting with friends, or contributing to the community?

The week progressed in typical fashion, with a mix of crises, gratifying outcomes, and a group therapy session which resulted in a client's admission that he had relapsed over Thanksgiving weekend. The group members were challenging but supportive and Lauren felt proud of them, and of herself, as she carefully led the group through several heated interactions.

She put away thoughts of being clinic director. God would guide her to the right decision. Until then, she would focus on her work.

Sally was one of the first to arrive at the pantry late Wednesday afternoon. As expected, the shift involved another intense upper body workout, (briskets, cabbages and black olives were provided to clients), in addition to some cardio when Lauren asked for her help with the children in the playroom.

"I remember how hyper the boys were the week before Christmas," Sally smiled. "I'd be glad to help." The children were easily corralled and agreed to sing carols until their parents' food orders were filled.

After cleanup, Sally stayed to talk to Lauren. Since they were both tired, she offered to buy Lauren a latte at the shop down the street. "Lauren, I don't want to intrude and I know I'm very new to the pantry. But I'm concerned about the limited inventory on the shelves. Will more food be arriving after the first of the year?"

Lauren hesitated. "I'm not supposed to say anything, Sally. Donations for all food banks in the area have been way down this year. Our director has hinted that the pantry may have to close, probably by the first of March, if things don't improve. And the problem's not just fewer food donations. We need hard cash to buy produce and specialty items."

"Again, please stop me if I'm imposing, Lauren, but I have lots of experience with fundraising. What have the executives at the food bank tried so far?"

"I think they've deferred planning until after the holidays," Lauren commented. "But the emails we get are pretty pessimistic. It's as if they think people are all tapped out or only giving to one favorite charity."

"How can I help? Sally asked. "My other causes

are running on autopilot and I've got ideas that could generate some quick cash."

Lauren studied Sally closely. The older woman had surprised her when they wrapped gifts together and again during the recent shifts at the pantry. She was, clearly, not the social butterfly Lauren had judged her to be. She was much more, a woman of depth.

As they sipped their coffees, Sally shared her fundraising expertise while Lauren listened in wonder. She especially liked Sally's idea of selling a heart-healthy cookbook using ingredients provided by the food pantry.

"But maybe you think that's too old fashioned," Sally fretted. "There are lots of cookbooks out there. One way to add interest might be to include a seasoning packet with each book. My trainer, Misty, has an organic herb and spice business. I bet she would donate some of her product to be a part of the publicity campaign."

"Let me run it by the director and she can check with her board," Lauren replied. "It also dovetails with another idea I had, involving helping pantry families with special occasion clothing. Their budgets don't allow for events like christenings, proms, and so forth."

"Hmmm, I like the way you think, Lauren. This is going to be fun!"

On Saturday, Lauren straightened her house while she tried to plan the evening's menu. She decided to feed Bryan from her monthly "clean out the pantry and freezer" accumulation. When her father was without work, Janice had instituted this tradition when money was scarce. The random food selection served to ease the budget and add creativity to the family meals, though sometimes "creative" was a nice way of saying "weird."

Choosing from the assortment of food, Lauren picked a half-full bag of frozen cheese ravioli, a block of pepper jack cheese, some hot sausage, and a jar of marinara sauce. Thinking the ingredients would be a nice combination of Italian and Mexican, she grated the cheese, cooked the sausage, layered everything in a casserole dish, and set it in the oven to bake. A loaf of garlic bread and a salad completed the meal. Dessert would definitely have to be something chocolate, and she was delighted when she found a close-to-expiring brownie mix in her pantry, which she supplemented with an almost empty bag of chocolate chips.

She wondered about her emphasis, which was almost compulsive at times, on frugal living. Was her father's past difficulty permeating her life, even now? Should she offer Bryan more than just this meal of discards? More importantly, was she avoiding her feelings for him by cooking a meal that was made of random ingredients?

Well, he would have to deal with it. Maybe she was testing him. Was he still the rich kid from high school, despite his concerns about the family business? She'd know soon.

Bryan arrived promptly at six, holding a bouquet of roses and a box of chocolate-covered strawberries. As usual, his eyes lit up when he smiled at Lauren. Even in a flannel shirt and jeans, he was as handsome as a television star. They hugged and

Lauren felt happier than she had in a long time. She vowed that the next time she cooked for him, if there were a next time, she'd do better.

Dinner was relaxed with Bryan insisting that he loved the ravioli bake, calling it an "interesting culinary fusion." They each discussed the years between high school and the present. Bryan described some wild times in college but noted he often felt lonely in a large group of people. Lauren talked of her sorority years, the many friends she had made, and her own feelings of isolation when her father was unemployed. After dinner, they brought their coffees to the living room couch.

"I'm grateful Dad landed on his feet," she told Bryan. "I think those years have left their mark on me, though. I've been offered the position of clinic director but my first thought when Dr. Cheaney asked to see me was that I was going to lose my job."

"Whoa, congrats!" Bryan said pumping his fist. "What are you going to do?"

"Good question. Dr. Cheaney said the hours would be manageable and on-call would be only one week out of eight. I love volunteering at the food pantry and doing my sewing part-time. And I've got to admit that your offer to design for Mohr's has been on my mind as well. I guess this is one of those times I need to remember to put the decision in God's hands because I sure don't know what the right answer is."

Bryan paused, ignoring the reference to God's help with the decision. "That's a lot to consider, Lauren. I don't know the mental health world very well. Would you mind if I asked a few questions?"

"Sure, go ahead."

Inhaling deeply, Bryan said, "Well, at first the idea of one week in eight for on-call sounds good. But I wonder if you won't be more stressed since you'll be covering clients from all the clinics. You won't know their histories and so on. And you've told me before that even when you're not on call, your therapists will phone you for consultation when they're unsure about what to do with a crisis patient."

"Good points, all of them," Lauren said. "For not knowing much about mental health, you know a lot, Dr. Dawson!"

"One other thing," Bryan continued. "We're just getting to know each other better and I'm a little jealous of the demands a new job might make on you."

Lauren smiled, pleased and excited. "I'm glad you said that. I feel the same way. I'm not sure how we got off to such an antagonistic start but this feels a lot better!"

Bryan leaned in and gave Lauren a tender, lingering kiss. Her arms wrapped lightly around his neck and the kiss continued. As she broke away, she was embarrassed and blushing.

"You smell like Chanel No. 5," Bryan said. "A classic fragrance, very fitting for you. I like your style of combining current trends with the old standards. I sound like a retail geek but it's what I do for a living."

"Well, I've never thought of you as geeky," Lauren said. "It is unusual a man would identify a specific scent. I've always loved it, ever since high school, when I saved up for the smallest size they made. I rationed my perfume squirts for special occasions only."

More kissing resulted, with Bryan saying that he was glad this was a special occasion. Lauren pulled away, trembling.

"What's wrong?" Bryan teased. "I thought that was wonderful, not something to be stopped so soon."

"I haven't been kissed like that in a while," Lauren admitted. "It was wonderful but also unsettling. We don't want to go too fast with all this."

"I'm not sure what too fast means," he replied softly. "I'd be happy if we were seeing each other every day but, obviously, you have doubts about being with me."

Lauren was upset at his interpretation of her reaction to the kiss. "I don't think that's fair, Bryan," she said hotly. "You don't know what it's like to be let down by someone you trusted."

"Maybe I do," he said harshly. "Looks like this evening has played itself out. I'd better go."

Bryan drove home angry and, oddly for him, sad. He wondered what it would take to break through Lauren's defenses. More than that, he doubted she would ever let go of the desire to make Doug the man of her dreams. His sense of Lauren's personality was that she was somehow determined to recapture the feelings of first love she had with Doug, despite his ugly actions while they were together.

Maybe she was the one who needed counseling, instead of providing it to others. But he knew he had to let her find her way in their new relationship. He wondered if he had the time, or patience, to allow that to happen. Clearly, his temper had gotten in the way tonight.

Finding no comfort in these thoughts, he went home and continued to work on the business tasks his father had assigned him at the start of the fall season. Given the dark predictions from the consultants about brick-and-mortar retail businesses, Bryan struggled to discover ideas that would take Mohr's toward a successful bottom line.

He wished Lauren could help him with all this. But she would assume he was only with her for her business ideas or sewing skills. How could he get through to that woman?

After Bryan left, Lauren expressed her frustration by polishing her dining room table to a high gloss. Bryan just didn't get it. Why couldn't he see what Doug had done to her and to her ability to open up to someone new? And what was with her victim thinking? She sounded like someone in a soap opera!

As she calmed down, though, she admitted it wasn't just Bryan's fault for the evening's frustrating conclusion. Maybe she was hanging on to the dream of what she and Doug could have been. She had always hated losing. Supervisors in her master's program had repeatedly challenged her competitive nature. Losing Doug was humiliating at the most primal level. Her fear that she had not been good enough for him tapped into her deepest insecurities.

Even now, she admitted her sense of competition was intruding in her decision about accepting the clinic director job. The idea of being director had the main appeal of not having to answer to another therapist. It would be nice to be in charge for a change. But a quality director would be thinking about ways to make the clinic better for clients. A good director would have goals in mind for the future of the program. She hadn't thought of any ways the clinic could better serve patients. She had only pondered the pros and cons of the new position as they related to her best interest.

Ideas formed as she forced herself to think about new possibilities for the clinic. Tele-health was burgeoning. Serving rural clients via secured Internet video connections could enhance therapy results while also improving therapists' productivity hours. More outreach programming, including tables at the county fair, home shows, or retiree facilities, could help those reluctant to seek counseling by normalizing the process and meeting counselors in person. The new director could also convince administration to tally outreach time as direct service to patients, a continued area of contention between therapists and those in charge.

As she brainstormed ideas, which she admitted were good, Lauren realized she wasn't all that enthused about any of them. What she really wanted was a private practice. She wanted to set her own hours, have enough time for the food pantry, and time to sew. No, create. She also had to make an adequate salary to live on which she probably should have listed first when she started thinking about all this.

Lauren went to bed but couldn't sleep. After two frustrating hours of tossing and turning, she got up. "Just like I tell my clients with insomnia to do," she said aloud to the silent house. Putting on some of her favorite music, she opened her Bible to her favorite passages. The verses about trusting God, forgiveness, and giving to others convicted her. The conviction, however, was comforting in its way, helping her to renew her resolve to live her life the way God intended.

After church the next day, the idea of a private practice continued to crystallize. Lauren's thoughts filled with possibilities. In the space of less than an hour, she had several rental offices in mind, along with plans for seating, design, and marketing strategies.

After her initial excitement, she paused. She'd always had private practice in the back of her mind but Doug wouldn't hear of it. "Too much financial risk," he'd always said. In hindsight, she realized that Doug had relied on her steady income and health benefits since he changed jobs so often. On her part, she had been willing to let him silence her dream.

Other memories of Doug intruded. When she had brought up the possibility of having children after they married, he deflected her with an assortment of excuses, some of which were legitimate. "We've both got school loans to pay," he would argue. "And we'll never get into the housing market if we add the expense of children."

Memories kept returning like a pesky Indiana mosquito. Doug had chosen their vacation destinations (always the beach, never the historical sights Lauren loved), their choice of restaurants (upscale chains for him, not local pubs for her), and the décor of the apartment they were to share after the wedding (his stark modern style won out over her homey floral prints).

Lauren had another "a ha" moment as she recalled these patterns. Again and again, she had given in. Whatever Doug said or wanted, she'd agreed to. In her work life, she was assertive and confident but not with Doug. She was so intent on getting married she had lost her sense of self. She'd gotten lazy in the relationship, allowing her hopes of a perfect future cloud her judgment.

Well, Doug wasn't a consideration now. She could afford no-frills health insurance. She had her little house and she would eat beans every meal if she had to. Furnishing an office would be simple. She would need only a desk, laptop, and two comfortable chairs. She realized she would do anything to make this dream come true. Bryan Dawson was part of her dream for the future, too. She was determined to figure that out as well. It was time to be a grown-up. No more Cinderella thinking. It was time to be her own Fairy Godmother.

Chapter Ten

Per Tom's orders, Bryan spent the rest of the week-end dealing with the resurrection of Mohr's. Those consultants had been useless. Doubling his frustration was the fact that his father hadn't listened when Bryan told him their fees would be a waste of money.

Like his mother, however, Bryan wasted little time dwelling on past mistakes. He needed to find a creative way to save Mohr's. Closing the store was a last resort but he realized keeping it open in its present form was impossible. The store could no longer offer everything to everybody in tiny Gordon. Costs were too high. Given the new big box store only twenty minutes away, customers could find most of what they needed, even groceries and medications.

So what did Mohr's do that no one else could replicate? Bryan ticked off Mohr's specialties in his head: great customer service, high-quality clothing, special orders with no risk or extra charge, easy access, familiarity.

As he had in the last several weeks, he longed for Lauren's input. She was the creative one, not him. Just look at the dress she'd designed and sewn for Jenny's wedding. It rivaled the gowns at the designer stores Bryan visited on buying trips. If only he could tell her, without her assuming his only interest in her was for the business! Or for sex! He set his jaw and decided to try again. Lauren was too important to him to leave things unsettled.

When he called, Lauren picked up on the first ring. She sounded happy to hear from him. She was open to discussing his plans for Mohr's, after he repeatedly said that he wanted to see her soon, no matter what they talked about.

"I'd love that, Bryan," Lauren said. "You'd be surprised at what Sally and I have been up to in the last few weeks. I want to tell you about that too."

"Sally! As in my mom? Are you kidding?"

"No kidding, Bryan. Your mom is great, actually wonderful. She's one of the pantry's best volunteers and she's going to head a fundraising drive for us in February. Without her help, it's likely that the pantry will close by mid-year."

"You didn't tell me anything about that," Bryan said accusingly. "I'd like to help too."

"I'm sorry for holding out on you. But it seemed hypocritical to discuss the pantry's problems when I was accusing you of using me to help Mohr's! And our last date ended awkwardly too."

"So we start again. Deal?" Bryan held his breath as he waited for Lauren's answer.

"Deal!"

Bryan and Lauren had dinner at her house the next evening. She was grateful for her trusty slow cooker since the day at the mental health center had been loaded with walk-ins and crisis calls. Chicken with wine sauce, rice pilaf, and a salad made for a simple but elegant feast. Conversation focused on Mohr's, with many possible solutions generated. None seemed feasible for the long-term, frustrating them both.

"Well, we solved nothing but I enjoyed every minute," Bryan said as they sat together on the sofa, drinking coffee. He leaned in and kissed Lauren gently at first, then more heatedly.

Lauren had thought a lot about their previous kisses and her negative reaction to them. Tonight, she was convinced Bryan had no agenda other than being in a relationship with her and she responded slowly, tempering his intensity. After several delicious moments, they broke apart and looked happily at each other.

Lauren broke the silence. "Dawson, you know all about my fiasco of an engagement with Doug but I know nothing of your romantic history. Spill!"

Bryan was silent for several seconds, causing Lauren to wonder if she'd pushed too hard. A look of sadness crossed his handsome features. "I guess you have a right to know but I hate talking about her. Her name was Angela. We were together during our MBA program. It was a good relationship, at first, but when we graduated she insisted that we move to New York. I understood that she had lots of ambition but when she called Mohr's 'that dead-in-the-water relic,' I realized how different we were."

Lauren ached for Bryan and felt a surge of anger at Angela. "What a snob!" she exclaimed. "As my mother would say, you deserve better!"

"Maybe Angela was right. Mohr's is sinking fast. We were counting on the holiday shopping surge to even out the year's sales total but it hasn't surfaced. For the first time in my life, I'm dreading the New Year. It's a void. There's no way to predict what's going to happen."

"That's always true, isn't it?" Lauren asked quietly. "We think we have things all mapped out but life interferes. Every year when I fill out my planner with my loved ones' birthdays, I wonder what the year will bring for each person. And sure enough, there's no way I can predict what actually happens. But then again, I really don't want a crystal ball either! God gets me through whatever occurs though I'll admit that, at times, my belief in His power is weaker than it should be."

"I agree that knowing ahead of time, about both the good and bad events in our lives, would be a huge burden. There would be no joy in life," Bryan said. "But I can't believe in God the way you do. I mean, I believe He exists but church isn't for me. Too much hypocrisy for my taste. Anyway, if your mom thinks I deserve better, I'm willing to go with that. Actually, I think I've found much better. What about you, Lauren?"

"I agree…. Maybe our pain with Doug and Angela helps us appreciate all this even more. And as the old saying goes, 'God works in mysterious ways!' What if our histories in bad relationships were preparation for a good one?"

She longed to ask for more specifics about Bryan's relationship with Angela but his obvious pain stopped her.

Enough for now, she thought. He's got scars, just as I do. The anguish in his face tells me all I need to know about his capacity for love. I've sold him short by assuming he could be casual about romance.

After leaving Lauren's house, Bryan settled in at home. Discussing Angela had been difficult and this rattled him. Why waste time thinking of her when he and Lauren were becoming closer? Because, he realized, he had loved Angela completely. Or he'd thought so at the time.

Angela Alcott was a powerhouse. She aced her MBA courses with minimal preparation while Bryan slaved away over term papers and case studies. She had the confidence to challenge professors, usually with good results. She was equally passionate in their relationship, alternatively sweet but then dismissive, even mean, especially with regard to Mohr's and Bryan's commitment to the family business.

Of course, her beauty lengthened his time in the relationship, which he was ashamed to admit. Bryan suddenly realized Angela's tall, blonde, California-surfer looks were the antithesis of Lauren's petite, dark, almost smoldering appearance. He could get lost in Lauren's eyes but he felt like he was home, and safe, with her. He sure hadn't felt safe with Angela. Excited and off-balance but never safe. Maybe he had to get the tempestuous glamour girl out of his system before he could appreciate real beauty.

He tried to stretch comfortably on his sofa, a continuous losing battle. Between its harsh lines and his long legs, no comfort was to be found. He looked around at the apartment and sighed.

He'd signed a lease too quickly after Angela refused to move to Gordon. Tom and Sally had almost begged him to live with them at the lake house but he craved his independence and privacy. In his rush, and because he'd been hurt and angry, he'd ordered all the furniture at once, selecting room packages that looked good in the catalog. Luke Sawyer, his old buddy and owner of the local furniture store, had suggested that Bryan go slowly, perhaps furnishing one room at a time, but Bryan had insisted on filling the apartment immediately. He should have trusted Luke. Luke risked a big sale by being a good friend. This place looks sterile. Perfect, but lifeless.

Steel gray colors, chrome lighting fixtures, and stock art on the walls provided no hint of the man living in the spacious apartment. The kitchen appliances, all professional series, had never been used, with the exception of the freezer and microwave. Bryan's master bedroom suite, with its gray tweed duvet covering the king-size bed, was filled with expensive black lacquered furniture.

Sally said it needed a woman's touch. She was probably right but there were no women lined up to help. Angela would have spent a fortune on designer pieces but he doubted he'd have liked the results. Even her apartment at grad school reeked of money. Who fancied up grad school rentals? Angela was the only one of their friends with a place fit for hosting the dean of the business school. Which she had, at her graduation party.

Lauren's place was cozy, though. She could work wonders with this apartment. But then she'd think he was out to take advantage of her, yet again. Since they'd had such a good evening, he didn't want to rock the boat. Not yet.

The mental health center hosted its annual holiday party on the last workday before Christmas. Since funds were so tight, the party was held in the central office, just outside of Indianapolis. Lauren drove solo, declining offers to car pool. She wanted to be able to exit quickly if the festivities weren't so festive.

The lobby was decorated with obvious care but did little for the low morale of employees. Lauren ran into Carol, a classmate from her master's program, who was now based at the main office. After hugs were exchanged, gossip began.

"What do you think about all the changes coming?" Carol asked.

"Not sure," Lauren said. "I'm just praying we can still meet the needs of our clients, without too much administrative interference."

"I hope your prayers work," Carol said darkly. "There's a rumor group therapy will be mandated prior to allowing clients to have individual sessions. Can you imagine the effects of that in the small towns we serve? It's hard enough to get folks to come to therapy, without them worrying about confidentiality leaks from group members who have been forced into participating."

"That would be awful!" Lauren said. "I don't think the risk is lack of confidentiality, though.

Clients just won't come to treatment, period. Worst case, it will spiral into fewer and fewer numbers of people served and more satellite center closures will result."

"Good point," Carol admitted. "Switching gears, what's new with you? Anyone in your life? Doug should be ancient history by now."

"If only," Lauren said with mock horror. "He showed up at my place, full of promises to make our relationship work again. And get this. He's been in counseling and it really helped him!"

Both women laughed and Carol was the first to speak. "I hate to put our profession down but, obviously, Doug's commitment to therapy is questionable. He was always a skilled manipulator."

Carol's personal life was next on the agenda with details of her new boyfriend and his recent job transfer comprising the rest of the social hour. After appetizers, the center's holiday bonus was distributed. A hush settled over the assembled staff as the envelopes were opened.

"What is this?" Carol whispered as she studied the check in the envelope. "I can't even buy a holiday ham with this paltry amount. I'm going to invest in lotto tickets. Maybe I'll double my money and buy two hams!"

Lauren agreed that the bonus was tiny and wondered silently about the future of the mental health center. Should she be considering the Gordon center directorship if clinical decisions were to be mandated by the main office? Financial stress had always been a reality at the center but this year's bonus indicated things were truly dismal.

On December twenty-third, Sally reviewed the menus for Christmas Eve and Day. Unlike past years, she planned to prepare the holiday food herself instead of relying on catering services to provide the meals. The important thing was that the family would be together. Funny how that mattered more than anything now. She had meant to ask Bryan if he was bringing anyone for Christmas dinner and she wondered if Lauren would be his date. This led to a review of their last talk at the pantry when Lauren had suggested helping families at the pantry with special occasion clothing.

Lauren was talented and smart. Her hand-crafted clothing won awards in high school. Sally smiled ruefully, remembering that viewing Lauren's designs was a welcome diversion from Bryan's numerous athletic events. Bryan was talented and smart, too. She wished those two could appreciate each other more. Something good was brewing between them but she sensed tension as well.

Sally's mind returned to the challenge of providing clothing items for the families served by the food pantry. One person wouldn't be able to meet the demand of the two hundred families served each week, but maybe 4-H clubs, Home Ec classes ("Is that what they're called now?" she wondered out loud to Izzy), or senior citizens clubs could.

Food and clothing are basic needs, Sally thought. If we could improve the quality of both, using the cookbook recipes and help from crafters, we could actually change lives.

Sally grinned at her grand thinking. But somehow, she felt energized and more hopeful than she had in months.

As with Thanksgiving, Christmas at the Gardner home was filled with tradition. After the early service at church, Lauren and her parents returned home for brunch. Egg-sausage casserole, fruit compote, and lots of coffee served as the prelude to unwrapping the gifts. The Gardners had a long-standing Christmas rule of a fifty-dollar spending limit per person with the rest of the Christmas budget being donated to the food pantry.

The spending limit always resulted in gifts that generated laughter and teasing. Lauren's father, Peter, received his obligatory necktie (found by Lauren on clearance for five dollars), T-shirts featuring slogans and references to the challenges of the teaching profession and subscriptions to his favorite magazines. Janice chuckled as she unwrapped several pieces of costume jewelry, saying, "You know I love my bling!"

Lauren received several items for her home. Luxurious bath towels, a high-speed blender, and a welcome mat for the front porch were among her stash of gifts. "Are you sure these total under fifty dollars?" Lauren asked. "I priced this blender at ninety-nine dollars a week ago."

"Honey, you've got to accept the benefits of being an only child," Janice said smoothly. "Let's just say that everything you got was on sale or clearance, so we still kept to the spirit of the fifty-dollar rule."

The threesome then worked together to prepare their traditional Christmas dinner. Ham, scalloped potatoes, salad, rolls, and Janice's huge assortment of holiday cookies left them all drowsy after the meal.

As they all cleaned the kitchen, Peter became serious. "We have so many things to be thankful for," he said. "The older I get, the more I realize our tough times have been blessings in disguise. If I hadn't lost those jobs, I'd never have explored teaching. Working with my students has been so rewarding. It's also meant a lot to me to have a teacher's schedule, so that I could be with my family."

"The schedule's good but the pay, not so much," Janice said wryly. "I agree though, Pete. At this point in our lives, it's not what you have, but who you have that makes all the difference."

Lauren studied her parents closely. What was going on here? Were they having health problems? Had they heard about her potential promotion? Or were they hinting at her relationship with Bryan? "Are you two okay?" she asked.

"Honey, we're fine," Janice said. "You know how sentimental your dad gets at Christmas. Nothing's up, really."

Lauren decided to discuss work since she didn't know where her relationship with Bryan was headed or even if they were in a relationship. "Funny you should focus on being with family, Dad," she said. "I've been offered the clinic director position but I'm having a tough time deciding if it's for me. My hours are long enough as it is."

The rest of the evening was spent discussing career options with her parents while carols played in the background. Pete offered cautionary input about the stressors of being director of the clinic. Janice, as usual, was an expert at providing "what if" and "what then" questions about the reality of being the day-to-day supervisor of a large mental health center.

"I love you two so much," Lauren said. "All you want is what's best for me. There's no pressure to be successful or to make you look good due to my professional position. I am truly blessed."

Peter and Janice looked at their daughter in surprise. "Of course we want what's best for you," Janice said. "We've been through enough in this life to know that you have to be true to yourself to be happy. Deep in your bones, you know that, too."

Peter chimed in. "I think you assume our expectations of you are higher than they are. Maybe we put too much pressure on you while you were in high school and college. Or maybe it's because you've been our only focus. But always know that if you're happy, we're happy."

At the Dawson home, Christmas veered from its usual high-end traditions. Absent were the Lenox china and linen napkins. The lack of catering meant Sally, (with the help of a few purchases made at the wholesale club), produced the meal. Despite the change, Bryan enjoyed the informality of the holiday. He had never been so relaxed with his parents.

"Sally, this is great," he said with his mouth full of bacon-wrapped shrimp while eying the platter of warm canapés and fresh vegetables. "The turkey smells fabulous. Did you get the caterer's recipe?"

Sally pretended to be insulted. "No, I did not. If you'll remember, I did all the cooking when you and your brother were little. This is my old, overnight slow-roasting recipe. It fills the house with the fantastic aroma of the holiday, doesn't it?"

Tom smiled at the banter between his son and wife. He missed his older son and his family but understood that travel to Gordon from New York was too expensive for them to afford every year. "You two are a hoot," he said to Bryan and Sally. "Just like old times, though I'm missing Jeff, Mandy, and the kids. Sometimes I wish I could freeze time and keep things just the way they are now."

Sally and Bryan exchanged a glance and then focused on Tom.

"Don't give me those looks," Tom said. "I'm fine and I sure don't want to talk business on Christmas Day. The New Year will come soon enough and we'll deal with our challenges then. In the meantime, what's for dessert after we eat this feast?"

"The food outlet cheesecake sampler," Sally retorted. "I'm a good meat and potatoes cook but Christmas baking gives me fits."

Bryan laughed and had the sudden awareness of how much he cared for his parents, despite his differences with them in the past. Tom's insistence that Bryan play every sport in high school, coupled with Sally's commitments to volunteer activities, had made him feel valued only when he achieved success. Time and maturity helped him realize his parents had done the best they could, given the pressures of growing the Mohr's brand.

Not that he would raise his kids the same way, though. Assuming he ever had any kids. Suddenly, the awareness that he wanted his own family around the holiday table struck him like a punch to the gut. An unfamiliar ache grew, an ache that spoke of emptiness and loss. He and Angela hadn't talked about having children but Bryan had assumed they would eventually. That dream was put to rest when she spoke so cuttingly about Mohr's future.

After dinner and clean up, Bryan called Lauren as he drove back to his apartment. "Merry Christmas," he said when she answered. "What are you up to?"

"Just relaxing after a lovely day and way too much food," she answered. "How was your holiday?"

"Best in years, actually. Tom and Sally were fun, though we missed Jeff and his family."

"That's wonderful, Bryan. You sound great."

"It occurred to me that we haven't celebrated by ourselves yet. How about lunch tomorrow?"

"Aren't you going to be busy with the after-Christmas sale at Mohr's?"

"Nope, this is my year off from the December twenty-sixth nightmare," Bryan said. "Bill is the manager in charge since he's taking New Year's week off for the wedding and honeymoon."

"I get it," Lauren said. "Well, if you're up for braving the crowds and indulging me in my quest for cheap Christmas cards and wrapping paper, I'd love to see you."

Downtown Gordon was a flurry of activity on the day after Christmas. Bryan and Lauren stopped at her favorite specialty shops, as she purchased half-price designer cards, gift bags, and a holiday wreath for her home.

"I'm all set for next Christmas," she said to Bryan. "Dawson, have I stretched your male shopping tolerance to the limit yet? I still have a gift card to cash in and I need new boots. I hear Mohr's is having a good sale."

Bryan winced. "We are having a good sale," he said. "But I'd like to steer clear of the store for today. You okay with that?"

"Sure, I was teasing," Lauren laughed. "Where should we have lunch?"

"After all the eating I've done in the last few days, I need something light. How about the Seafood Dock?"

At Bryan's suggestion, Lauren remembered their last meal at the restaurant, when she had been hurt by his idea that she design for Mohr's. "Yeah, that's a good idea," she said, thinking that her friendship with Bryan was more solid now.

"I promise, no business talk," Bryan said, reading her mind. "I want to hear all about your Christmas."

Lunch lasted two hours, with both Bryan and Lauren talking at length about Christmas traditions (and lack thereof) at each of their childhood homes.

"Mom and Dad spent too much on my gifts but, for the first time in several years, I think they're doing well financially. They've dug themselves out of the hole they were in when I was in high school," Lauren said.

"You went through a lot, didn't you?" Bryan asked. "I remember how serious you were all the time."

"Looking back, it was tough but character-building," Lauren said. "At the time, though, my eighteen-year-old self wished for more fun and less character!"

"I'm glad your parents are doing well, Lauren. They've shown a lot of grit. I think Tom and Sally are building character too. Sally nixed the catering service she's used for years and she prepared Christmas dinner on her own. She did a fine job, with good humor as well. I haven't seen Tom look at her with such tenderness in a long time."

Lauren was surprised at Bryan's admission of his parents' concerns. "That's really lovely, Bryan. Tom and Sally are quality people. Your mom has been a wonderful addition to the food pantry volunteer staff. I have one question, though. Why do you call them by their first names?"

Bryan paused before answering. "I think with my father, it became easier to call him Tom since we work together all day. I can't refer to him as Dad in meetings or on the sales floor. Our relationship at the store is sticky enough without being too casual on top of everything else."

Bryan took a deep breath and continued. "With my mother, it's more complicated. Maybe I need a good therapist to help me sort it out! I started calling her Sally to provoke her when I was twelve or so. She was never home and our housekeeper was more of a mother to me than she was. Then in college, I worked at the store during my breaks and summers off so I consistently called both of them by their first names."

"Well, as I say to my clients, families can be tricky," Lauren said. "You seem to have a pretty good take on why you call your parents by their given names so I'm not sure you need a therapist!"

Feeling courageous, Lauren continued. "That said, now that you're feeling closer to them, maybe you could call them Mom and Dad or whatever. It might mean more to them than you realize. Chances are they feel your distance when you call them by their given names."

"Maybe," Bryan replied. "I'm not sure if I can do it just yet. You're right. I have felt distant from them. Ironically, the crisis at the store has brought us all a bit closer. So we'll see."

Sensing Bryan's difficulty when talking about his parents, Lauren let the subject drop. After lunch, they took a walk through the grounds of the local community college. The trees in the park-like commons area were decorated with colored lights and several families were walking their dogs while their children played. Bryan took Lauren's hand in his while they strolled in silence.

"This is nice," Bryan said. "I forget how pretty this park is during the holidays. I'm usually too busy at the store to appreciate what Gordon has to offer. Once Mohr's is back on track, I hope we can see each other more often and enjoy our town."

Lauren's senses tingled as she and Bryan held hands. His openness about his relationship with his parents felt as intimate as their kisses. He trusted her with feelings she knew were hard for him to admit. Despite his past anger at his mother, his voice reflected only sadness and affection when he spoke of her.

She squeezed his hand and took her own emotional risk. "This is wonderful, Bryan. I love it when we can talk about our families and what's really important to us."

Bryan stopped and took Lauren in his arms for a tender, probing kiss. A group of pre-teen boys whistled and chortled, "Get a room!" They laughed and continued their walk.

"Where to next?" Bryan asked. "I vetoed going to Mohr's, so you get to choose."

"I'm shopped out for today," Lauren said. "Let's go to my place and you can help me take down some of the decorations that are too high to reach without a ladder. I'll pay for your work with ham-and-potato casserole for supper."

"So you only care for me because I'm tall," Bryan laughed. "I suspected as much but ham casserole sounds good. Sally made a delicious roast turkey yesterday but her skill with leftovers is limited. It will be turkey sandwiches until all the bird is gone."

Lauren marveled at Bryan's relaxed mood. At the same time, she was still afraid of becoming too close to him. What if the holiday and wedding activities were making them both too eager? The thought of committing to someone who could betray her as Doug had was frightening. As these thoughts crowded into her brain, she chided herself for her doubts. What more could she ask for in a man? Bryan was intelligent, kind, and very easy on the eyes. Despite his professed doubts about God, he had a profound sense of right and wrong, along with a willingness to work hard for what he wanted. How could she compare him to Doug? They were complete opposites.

Back at Lauren's house, her fears dissipated as she and Bryan made quick work of the holiday decorations hung above her fireplace and over her front door. The tree, table centerpiece, and Christmas kitchen décor were still intact but Lauren would be able to take those down by herself.

"Boy, you really love to decorate, don't you?" Bryan said. "Sally hires all this out and each year has a different theme. One year everything was silver and gold. It was pretty but I like your stuff better."

Giving Bryan the fisheye, Lauren retorted, "My collection of stuff is the result of years of acquisition, buddy. Since you teased me about it, you now get to hear the history of each item!"

Lauren then described most of her Christmas decorations. The third-grade picture ornament, featuring her with bangs cut in a zigzag line across her forehead, was Bryan's favorite. After he quit laughing, he said, "I don't have any personal photo ornaments but if I did, I'm not sure I'd keep one like this around."

"Not funny," Lauren smiled, in spite of herself. "My mom insisted on a quick trim the night before class pictures and she, obviously, had dull scissors and a shaky hand. I endured lots of teasing after pictures came out that year but Jenny was a loyal friend. She even beat up a boy who called me 'Hacksaw.' He was afraid to go out to recess for a full week!"

"I'd better be showing my future cousin-in-law more respect," Bryan grinned. "What's the story on this ornament?"

"This one was from my great-aunt," Lauren said, holding a tiny blown-glass Christmas tree. "She was a free spirit, traveled the world, and never married. This ornament is from a glass factory in Venice. When she died, she left my parents some money that helped them catch up on bills when my dad wasn't working. But the thing I liked best about her was her strong faith. I'd go to her assisted-living apartment to provide her with some company, as my mother insisted. Aunt Abby would listen to all of my teen angst, then remind me that God loved me, no matter what. The visit was always about me, not her, but I think she liked it that way."

The rest of the afternoon was spent discussing the remainder of Lauren's ornament collection. Many of the trinkets were old and battered but each was described with love and memories.

"I envy your sense of tradition," Bryan said. "Our tree, or trees, depending on Sally's mood each year, are strictly designer affairs. As I said, one year everything was silver and gold, another year pastels. Last year we had three trees, each done in Indiana themes – the 500, Colts, and Pacers. Not exactly the spirit of the season."

"It all sounds impressive," Lauren replied, without real conviction. "My style isn't for everyone either. Christmas is supposed to be personal if nothing else. But I'm wondering about a tree full of Colts ornaments! Was each player featured?"

Holiday clean-up was finished amid laughter and Christmas music. Lauren went to the kitchen to assemble the casserole, adding extra cheese and onion for depth of flavor. Bryan trailed behind her, again praising her home. "Your kitchen is just big enough," he said. "The appliances are arranged well with everything within arm's reach. Did you design this?"

"No, the builder in 1949 did," Lauren said with a chuckle. "Kitchens were much smaller then, so everything was within arm's reach by necessity."

Bryan set the table, using Lauren's Christmas

dishes. "Where did you get these?" he asked. "I've never seen this pattern at Mohr's."

"Nope, you won't find it at Mohr's," Lauren responded. "I collected it piece by piece, when I was in college, from a grocery store promotion. Just as I finished completing a basic set for four, the store went out of business. If you look closely, you'll see the bowls and bread plates don't match the rest of the set. I read last year that mixing china patterns is now very chic, so I'm going with it!"

Dinner was lighthearted and dishwashing quick. Afterwards, Lauren and Bryan sat on her sofa. She put her head on his shoulder and he drew her near. Their kisses escalated quickly and, this time, there were no obnoxious teens to shout that they should get a room.

Lauren tried to catch her breath but didn't want the kissing to end. Bryan was equally passionate, wrapping his arms around her waist more and more tightly, pulling her into his body as he leaned back on the armrest of the sofa. As she leaned into him, he stroked her face and then moved his hands down her neck and shoulders.

Lauren broke away. "Bryan, we have to take it easy," she said breathlessly. "This isn't about Doug or anyone else, it's about me. Do you understand?"

Bryan looked at Lauren's anguished face, her green eyes cloudy. "I understand but I don't like it. I think your religious dogma is getting in our way. You're an adult woman with normal desires. This isn't wrong. We care about each other!"

He plowed on, filled with the anger of frustration and rejection. "And doesn't the Bible say to go forth and multiply? Or something like that?"

"So now we're multiplying?" Lauren said scornfully. "You're a hard one to figure out, Dawson. First we have normal desires, then we're ready to pop out some kids!"

After allowing herself to calm down, she continued. "Wait, I didn't mean to be harsh. It's easy for me to get mad when I'm feeling misunderstood. What I need for you to believe is that sex is very important to me. Doug was unfaithful and at times I wonder if it's because we were waiting until we got married to be intimate. But I couldn't change his attitude. I've tried to be different about sex but I always get back to the same place. I want to be sexual with my husband, not my boyfriend. I don't think it's fair to label that belief dogma."

"And now I'm being punished for Doug's failures? Bryan asked. "You think that I would, or could, betray you the way he did? Wow, we don't really know each other at all."

He stood up, grabbed his coat and walked to the door. "It's been a great day, Lauren. It could have been a great night as well. See you at the rehearsal dinner."

Lauren shook the tears from her eyes. She hated that Bryan disagreed with her feeling about being with him. He probably thought she was trying to trap him into marriage. Then she became angry. Her values were important to her and if Bryan Dawson couldn't understand that, so be it.

Working at the mental health center exposed her to many different value sets. More often than not, clients made the best choices they could and Lauren worked with them on clarifying their beliefs as they grappled with decisions about impulsivity, sex, and relationships. At least if she ended up in private practice, she could be more open about her Christian orientation.

So if I have my own practice, I can share my beliefs. But sharing them with the man I love gets me nowhere. Pondering that conundrum, Lauren went to bed.

Fidgeting on his sofa at home, Bryan raged at Lauren's reluctance to get closer to him. He realized that he wanted to go to bed with her as a way to express his feelings but her ideas about sex were antiquated and required marriage first. It was the classic male/female dichotomy. Men wanted to be sexual to express closeness and women wanted to be emotionally close before they had sex. Or was that just psychobabble? He wasn't sure and he was too irritated to think it through.

She seemed so sophisticated. Mental health work meant having a tolerance for others' choices and he was sure she had heard about all kinds of different lifestyles. It didn't fit with how she was reacting to him at all.

But then he realized he was as rigid in his choices as Lauren. He was as unaccepting of her beliefs as she was of his. If he really cared for her and he realized he did, he would have to take things slowly. Even more slowly. Hopefully, it wasn't too late for them.

The twenty-seventh dawned clear and cold. As she lingered in bed, Lauren resolved to connect with Bryan before the rehearsal dinner. What was the point of celebrating the wedding of the dearest people in their lives while they themselves were filled with anger? She decided to call Bryan this evening after she ran errands.

Despite her insistence that the gown and veil were her wedding gifts to Jenny and Bill, Lauren wanted to buy them something else, something personal. Since Bryan had the week off at the store, she decided it was safe to start her gift hunt there.

Mohr's aisles were still decked out in their Christmas splendor. Lauren would miss the cheerful bows and ornaments but she also loved having four seasons. She could already anticipate the daffodils blooming in a few months. After checking Jenny's registry list, Lauren was at a loss. Every single item had been purchased.

Lauren wandered to the home section of the store. Her eyes lit up when she saw it, a beautiful cross, encrusted with pastel crystals. It would be perfect for Jenny and Bill's home, symbolizing their commitment to God and to each other. She went to the register and was startled by a familiar voice behind her.

"Thought you needed boots," Bryan said smoothly.

"And I thought you were off today," she responded. "Although I was going to call you after I got home."

"Well, you've got me now. I am off. I just wanted to see what the post-Christmas crowd was looking like."

"It was kind of personal," Lauren stammered. Looking around and seeing no one nearby, she continued. "I hated the way last night ended. You're too important to me to let you think that I have any agenda. My beliefs about marriage are probably too old fashioned for a man like you but I wanted you to know I care deeply for you."

"Let's go to my office," he said, taking her hand.

When they reached the office, which was just down the hall, Bryan hugged Lauren in a long embrace. She felt cherished and accepted although he hadn't responded to her concerns about the previous evening. She was glad she had been honest even if it meant that Bryan would end their relationship.

He surprised her with his next words. "I care for you too, Lauren. No, I think I love you, which I can't believe I'm saying. And I should have been more respectful of your beliefs. Maybe with time, we'll both compromise a little."

Lauren's happy bubble burst at that statement. "Compromise? What does that mean? How would that work? And you think you love me but you can't believe you've said it. I think I should be heading home." She squared her shoulders and left the office with dry eyes, for a change. At least he wouldn't see her cry this time.

Bryan gazed at Lauren's back. He knew she meant what she said about him being important to her. She was being transparent, honest, and true. But there she went again as he watched her navigate the crowded store displays. No matter what he said, it was wrong. He'd never had this much trouble communicating with a woman. Of course, communication with Angela was handled with fewer words and more action. How was he going to get through to Lauren if saying he loved her wasn't enough? He did love her. Somehow, though, his message came across as manipulative and gamey. What next?

Chapter Eleven

The Newton Rustic Getaway was nestled in a woodsy area on the Wabash River, about a two-hour drive from Gordon. Log cabins were available for family rentals while the main lodge housed individual rooms, a gourmet restaurant, a full-service spa, and an indoor pool. A walking trail highlighted Indiana beauty, regardless of the season. The river, flowering plants, vines, and rock arrangements ensured numerous photo-ops.

Members of Jenny's wedding party gathered at noon in the main dining room for the first part of the bachelorette party, enjoying a lunch of grilled salmon on mixed greens. Dessert was an assortment of fresh fruit with a splash of sparkling wine.

"If all the meals for the next twenty-four hours are like this, you'll have to double-wrap the sash on my gown," Jenny whined. "After the last few weeks of Christmas goodies, this is like starvation rations."

"You'll feel better after a massage," Lauren said. "I'm headed to the masseuse now. We all meet at five for pre-dinner spritzers. Be prepared for mucho embarrassment. I've told the girls to tell every silly story they have from their friendship with you."

"I'm planning on a long nap and a short walk around the grounds," Jenny said. "I may also have to make a quick trip to the gas station down the road for a candy bar or two. See you at five."

The spa was beautifully appointed. Muted shades of cream, gold, and peridot green ensured an atmosphere of relaxation and peace. Lauren's massage room had a view of the river, allowing her to see the sycamore trees sway in the late December wind.

Lauren met her masseuse, Mai, and prepared to enjoy the bliss of complete relaxation. After about ten minutes of deep shoulder and back massage, though, she began to feel weepy.

"You okay, honey?" Mai asked. "You're tightening up. Are you crying?"

"I don't know what's wrong with me," Lauren said. "I've been looking forward to this for a long time."

"Not to worry," Mai said. "It happens. People with lots on their minds, lots of stress on the job and so forth, often get this way as their muscles release the pent up emotional energy. We can stop if you want or I can do a head and shoulder massage in the chair."

"Let's do the chair," Lauren said. "I have had a lot going on lately."

The chair massage was pleasant, enabling Lauren to relax a little. She tried to empty her mind, with little success. She remembered Bryan's easy chatter as they put away her Christmas decorations, along with his unspoken longing for more stability in his life. Thoughts of Bryan's kisses, Bryan holding her, and then her recent angry exit from Mohr's kept intruding.

Can't wait for the next few days. We'll be together practically nonstop. What a mess I've made of things! Lauren's thoughts tightened her muscles the minute she left the massage room.

Thankfully, Jenny was none the wiser about Lauren's unhappy massage. Jokes, embarrassing stories, and fond memories filled the early evening. The bridal party then enjoyed a substantive supper, much to Jenny's relief. Sauces of every kind smothered the chicken, fish, and pork offered on the buffet line. Side dishes were heavy in starches, scant in green vegetables, and the sole healthy ingredient in the dessert tray was dark chocolate.

Two days later, Jenny and Bill's rehearsal dinner was held at the country club just outside the Gordon city limits. The old building had been recently renovated but continued to exude old money and class. Since the Sturms were paying for the dinner, Mavis made sure everything was top-of-the-line. The surf and turf entrée included a mini filet mignon with lobster tail, the meal concluding with a dessert of baked Alaska.

"Can't beat this for an upper crust shindig," Jenny's mother said. "Those Sturms are growing on me. Mavis even complimented me on Jenny's frugal ways. At first, I thought she was being sarcastic but she was sincere."

Lauren smiled in response. "I think the

Sturm-Dawson clan is made up of quality people," she said. "But it takes a while to get to know them."

"Yeah, Mavis is okay, Mom," Jenny said. "And I was ready for real food after that spa cuisine. I lost two pounds in twenty-four hours! Lauren sure knows how to pamper a bride! And that was sarcasm in case you didn't get it!"

Lauren laughed. "As I recall, you really enjoyed supper, Jenny. And the spa was your idea. You vetoed a stripper, remember?"

"As if," Jenny said, with a dramatic eye-roll. "Not my cup of tea at all."

After dinner, the wedding party went out for dancing. Lauren and Bryan intentionally avoided each other, chatting with the other attendants the whole evening. Lauren danced with the groomsmen while Bryan boogied with every bridesmaid. Lauren watched covertly as Bryan showed off his best dance moves. He was such a player. How could she have thought he was any different than Doug?

New Year's Eve certainly had a different character this year. Instead of going to parties with friends, Lauren and Jenny were busy with last-minute wedding details. The rehearsal dinner had taken place the night before, due to New Year's Eve bookings at the country club.

"I thought the dinner and rehearsal went well," Lauren commented to Jenny, as they inspected the church decorations. The Christmas poinsettia floral arrangements already in place were complimented by Jenny's addition of white rose clusters, baby's breath, and glittered ferns.

"Yeah, they were fine," Jenny replied. "I was nice to Mavis and I told her that my dress was an ivory shade and very traditional." Jenny's concerned look belied her comment.

"So what's wrong?"

"Mavis confided in me that Mohr's is in deep trouble," Jenny said. "I knew sales were off but I had no clue that Bill and Bryan could lose their jobs if the store has to close. I was floored when she told me, especially after the feast they provided for the rehearsal dinner. No wonder she's admiring my budgeting skills."

Unwilling to betray Bryan's confidence about Mohr's, Lauren asked, "What are they going to do? Are there any options to keep Mohr's alive?"

"Mavis said the consultants weren't very optimistic or helpful. She said they need a brilliant idea to establish a unique identity in a small town like Gordon." Jenny's tone matched her gloomy statement.

Lauren's stomach tightened. There it is again. Are my special occasion dresses the brilliant idea?

Jenny studied her friend. "You've got your pinched face on again, Lauren. You give yourself away every time. Mavis said nothing about Bryan's thought of using your designs at Mohr's. Don't go assuming that he's going to ask you about that again."

"I wasn't," Lauren lied. "But on to more exciting things. Tomorrow, at this time, you'll be a married woman!"

New Year's Day dawned clear and cold. Lauren woke with a sense of sadness. She surveyed her cozy bedroom, its décor reflecting relationships, family, and love. Another year begins with me as a single woman. And I'll be watching my best friend get married. I'm happy for Jenny but I'll admit, I'm really envious.

Coupled with her envy of Jenny's happiness was Lauren's anxiety about the job offer at the clinic. Did she want to be a director? Was the financial security worth the hassle? On the other hand, did she want to be pinching pennies for the rest of her life?

As her father said often when he was unemployed, it was time to really crunch the numbers. Lauren spent the morning working on a spreadsheet detailing her income and expenses for the last twelve months. She also estimated start-up, malpractice insurance, and marketing costs for a private practice. She'd played with the numbers before but had never put them down in black and white or in such detail.

Well, she'd said she would eat beans if she had to and they would have to be the inexpensive dry kind, not canned. Maybe she could add instant ramen noodles, when they were on sale, for an occasional treat. The projections weren't good but they weren't impossible either. Perhaps the beginning of a New Year was the time to branch out on her own. The more she thought about being clinic director, the more trapped she felt.

Other options surfaced as Lauren thought about her future. What if she took the director's job for a limited time, like a year, and saved the excess salary for a private practice start-up fund? That would give her a solid financial base to supplement her current savings account which was pretty lean.

While this plan had merit, Lauren's stomach

tightened at the thought of directing the clinic, even on a short-term basis. She was always telling her clients to trust their instincts. Maybe it was time she did the same.

The afternoon was filled with happy chatter in the church's back room as Jenny, Lauren, and the rest of the bridesmaids had their hair and makeup done. Lauren was startled when she saw herself in the mirror. The makeup artist had highlighted her dark good looks, using an eye shadow that emphasized her hazel eyes and ivory skin. Her thick, dark-brown hair had been gently waved and swept into a partial updo.

Maybe it was true that you needed to style yourself for the man you wanted, just as you should dress for the job you wanted. If her goal was to be married this time next year, she should tend more to her makeup, and dress more fashionably, even sexy. This thought didn't last long, however. She was always telling clients to be themselves. What was the point of being someone you weren't? Life was too short to play those games. She could look nice and still be herself.

Jenny walked over to admire Lauren's makeup. Jenny's anxiety from yesterday had, obviously, left her and she was the typical happy bride-to-be. She spoke quietly as they waited for the wedding march to begin.

"You look terrific, Lauren. Thanks for glamming up for the wedding. I know you're more comfortable with the natural look. By the way, I gave myself a good butt-kicking last night," she told Lauren.

"Even if Mohr's closes, Bill is a great businessman and I've got my teacher's salary to help us get by. We may eat beans a lot but we can do it."

"Sounds like we're thinking alike, yet again," Lauren said, laughing as she hugged her friend. She told Jenny about her renewed focus on leaving the clinic to start a private practice.

"Do it," Jenny said firmly. "I can't believe it's taken you so long to realize this. It's a no-brainer. You're ready for the independence. You need a chance to craft your therapeutic style without the hassles of the agency's red tape."

As Jenny proceeded down the aisle, her beauty struck Lauren. Her gown, which Lauren hadn't seen in a few weeks, looked wonderful. The beaded trim on the shoulders and veil headpiece sparkled in the golden candlelight. Despite Jenny's protests of starvation at the spa, the gown draped perfectly on her curvy frame. The effect was just as Jenny said she wanted when they met the first time to plan the gown. Simple and elegant.

Bridesmaids were dressed in equal simplicity, their gowns in cranberry satin with sweetheart necklines. Groomsmen sported black tuxedos with red rose boutonnières.

Lauren gazed at Bryan across the front of the church. His muscular body filled out his tuxedo without looking too macho. His blond hair was parted on the side and casually brushed back. Lauren noted that he could wear any color or style and look good. Only Bryan Dawson could get away with looking equally great in ripped jeans or a tux.

It just wasn't fair.

The wedding proceeded smoothly, with most guests becoming tearful as Jenny and Bill recited their personally written vows. After the ceremony, several guests in the receiving line commented about Jenny's gown, with Mavis often interjecting that the dress was "one of a kind."

"Did you tell Mavis I made the dress?" Lauren whispered during a lull in the line.

"Yep, I told her after the rehearsal dinner. I started by just saying it was a handmade ivory gown. She was panicked at the thought of a home-sewn dress but Sally overheard and went on and on about your sewing awards in high school. She said she was sure the dress would be gorgeous and it is! And by the way, Bryan was standing next to his mom and heard everything."

Lauren had to admit that Jenny had a point. Maybe this was a message from above. She could add to her income by crafting beautiful dresses, while she worked to build a private practice. She said a silent prayer to God, asking Him to make it so.

"This wedding is one of the happiest I've ever attended," Lauren told Jenny after the cake was cut. "Your mom and Mavis have gotten closer since the shower. I've heard several people say how much they enjoyed the pasta bar. The cake is delicious. You've had a great wedding, on your own terms. Good for you!"

As Lauren reflected on the beautiful wedding and its loving participants, someone tapped on her shoulder. "We haven't danced yet," Bryan said. "You've slow-danced with every groomsman except me."

Lauren smiled and slipped into Bryan's arms. The music segued into a romantic set, allowing the couple to hold each other close. Lauren rested her head on Bryan's shoulder, relishing the tenderness of the moment. Her movements blended with his as they swayed around the dance floor. At the end of the song, each was startled when a fast drumbeat began. They walked hand in hand to the bridal party table, which was empty now that the music was loud and current.

"We haven't really talked in a few days," Bryan said, deliberately ignoring the reason for this. "Anything new at work?"

"It's slow during the week between Christmas and New Year. I just take calls from home," Lauren said. "Are you really asking about my decision whether to accept the director's job?"

"Yes, I was actually. Have you made up your mind?"

"Not yet," Lauren said slowly. "It makes sense financially to take the promotion, while I save every extra cent for at least a year before I try to launch a private practice. But at what cost? I know in my heart that I'm a clinician, not an administrator."

"Stability is important, though," Bryan commented. "A regular income means a lot these days."

Lauren's eyes widened. She looked away. Once again, he sounded like Doug. Was he counting on her salary if they ever become a couple and Mohr's had to close? Was she back in the same place as with Doug, her income being the saving grace of the relationship? Did Bryan have so little faith in himself that he couldn't imagine getting another job if Mohr's closed?

"Gotta check on my bride," she said quickly. "See you later."

Bryan watched Lauren glide across the dance floor in search of Jenny. What was up with her now? At least with Angela, he knew where he stood. He was usually in trouble but he always knew what was going on, however unpleasant.

This wedding was really working on him. As he'd listened to Bill and Jenny recite their vows, he had been touched by the couple's assurance that they would manage life's challenges as a true team. That was another huge difference in his relationship with Angela. Teamwork had not been in their repertoire.

And as he danced with Lauren, Bryan remembered their kisses. She made him crazy. Even Angela hadn't caused this much frustration. Of course, he and Angela hadn't counted sexual frustration as one of their many problems because, in that area, she had taken charge. Bryan had been glad to let her. But in the end, their passionate relationship wasn't enough to override their differences. Oldest story in the book but since it was his book, he hadn't noticed.

The next day, battling his post-wedding fatigue and his confusion about Lauren, Bryan stared out his office window. The main street of Gordon's tiny downtown area was busy with shoppers. He wondered if the number of new purchases would outnumber the returns. His glum train of thought was interrupted when his phone buzzed. Gayle, his administrative assistant, asked to see him.

"Bryan, there's a Doug Mathas here to talk to you. He doesn't have an appointment but he says you two know each other." Gayle was a good judge of people and it was obvious that Doug was not passing her test.

"Doug Mathas? The only Doug I know would be…. Sure, show him in," Bryan said.

Doug entered the office with an extended hand which Bryan shook firmly. Each man studied the other. Doug spoke first.

"Thanks for seeing me, Bryan," he said cautiously. "I was obnoxious when we met at Lauren's and I apologize. I was holding out hope that she and I could get back together. But she's been very clear that it's not going to happen."

"What's on your mind today, Doug?" Bryan asked quietly, though he was thrilled to hear that Lauren had rebuffed Doug's attempts to reconcile. At least that part of her mysterious behavior was cleared up.

"Well, as I've told Lauren, I'm involved in a new sales venture, one that I think could be a good fit for Mohr's," Doug began. "In essence, we market coupon opportunities to local businesses and restaurants. When we compile a ten-coupon package, we mail it to women of a certain age in the surrounding counties. We target their birth month, when they're ready to treat themselves. Our marketing research shows return on investment for participating businesses is very good. The consumer market we target spends freely. It's a win-win for my company and yours if you decide to purchase our program."

"'Women of a certain age?' Sounds pretty condescending, Doug."

"My poor choice of words, Bryan. Our research shows that female Baby Boomers are great customers." Doug fidgeted in his chair.

"Tell me more," Bryan said, enjoying Doug's discomfort. "What kind of coupons?"

"Mohr's could tailor its own coupon offers, depending on what you want to market the most. For example, high-end steakhouses often offer twenty dollars off a minimum fifty-dollar purchase. The offer reads like a forty-percent discount but the average check at such restaurants is way over two hundred dollars for two people. So the restaurant basically gives away a couple of side dishes while making a nice profit on dinner. Mohr's could structure any sort of offer you'd like. You could provide a discount on lunch in the tearoom, or on a boutique purchase, or any combination that makes financial sense." Doug sat back in his chair, eying Bryan.

He could sell ice to an Eskimo. But it's an intriguing offer. Bryan paused, tapping his pen on the desk.

Bryan and Doug spent over an hour discussing terms of the coupon agreement. Bryan made plans to get back to Doug after he discussed the idea with his marketing director. The men parted cordially, Doug obviously grateful for the potential sale and with a new respect for Bryan's pointed questions about what the deal entailed.

As his car exited the Mohr's lot, Doug decided to call Lauren.

"What do you want, Doug?" she asked tersely.

"Nothing, really. Just wanted to fill you in on a meeting I just had with Bryan Dawson. He's considering an agreement to buy my newest product as a way to market Mohr's. Based on what I'm hearing that store could use the help," Doug said.

Lauren cringed at Doug's nasty tone. It was typical of him to want to brag at the expense of someone else. She deflected his baiting and asked, "What's that got to do with me, Doug? You seem to like your new sales job, and I'm glad for you, but please don't call me again."

"I thought, mistakenly perhaps, you'd appreciate not being surprised if you heard about my deal with Mohr's. It was simply a friendly call, nothing else."

Lauren stuck her tongue out at the phone but was determined not to engage in the game playing Doug enjoyed so much. She forced herself to smile. Wasn't that supposed to make a person's voice sound happy? She thanked Doug for his friendly gesture. Then, without letting him respond, she ended the call.

Later that day, Bryan talked to Lori, his marketing director, to discuss Doug's coupon offer.

"I've heard about this approach before," Lori said. "Mathas likely owns a franchise for this product. It's been all over Indianapolis and it's been fairly successful there. But Doug's got quite a different customer base in our rural area. He's in for some tough selling."

"Whatever," Bryan said. "Here's my question. Is this a good deal for Mohr's? And if so, once we increase the number of customers through the door, what then? How do we get them to buy and keep buying? We always end up at the same place. How do we emphasize the special things about Mohr's so that we can improve revenue?"

Lori paused and took a deep breath. "I can read between the lines, Bryan. I know Mohr's holiday numbers were bad. I owe it to you to tell you that I've got feelers out for jobs in Indy. Since the divorce, I'm relying on my income alone. I can't afford to be unemployed for long."

As he walked back to his office, Bryan thought that perhaps Lori wasn't the only one who should be looking for a job. After work, he stopped at the grocery on his way home. He was out of nearly everything and had been surviving on take-out and corn chips. Good thing he could handle stress in a healthy way. Not. Maybe he and Tom should just let Mohr's close with dignity.

As his jumbled thoughts bounced around in his mind, though, he became angry. No, he wasn't giving up on Mohr's. There had to be a way to reinvent their brand, a way to thrive in the twenty-first century. Too bad he couldn't figure out how.

At the clinical meeting following their last session, Lauren presented Penny as her case for input from her coworkers. She briefly summarized their work together, noting that Penny's mother would be attending next week's session.

"Typical oppositional-defiant disordered teen,"

said Kristen, the center's newest counselor. "She's setting you up to interact with her mother so she doesn't have to. Once Mom's exploring her own childhood conflicts, the heat will be off Penny and she'll do what she wants with her friends."

Kristen was anxious to be accepted by the older, more experienced counselors. She was eager to label and diagnose clients she had never met, not having learned yet that diagnosis was only the first step involved when helping a person in pain. Her inexperience also manifested itself by her unique choices in work clothing. Today, she was dressed entirely in black, even down to her black-framed glasses. Since Kristen wore contact lenses, everyone knew the glasses were part of the outfit.

"No, I see a budding character disorder," Ricky said. Ricky was a seasoned therapist who, in Lauren's opinion, tended to look down on the younger counselors. She also tended to pathologize every client behavior. She dressed in designer skirt suits and spike heels which Lauren thought put many patients off since their client base was largely middle class.

"Is she doing any cutting? How about eating disorder symptoms? Any needle tracks or does she keep her arms hidden? I doubt you thought to check for that." Ricky was on a roll and ready to hospitalize Penny without having ever met her.

Dr. Cheaney weighed in next. "What does Penny want, Lauren? What does she want from you, her mother, and her friends? I think there's an underlying agenda here and that purple hair, a smart mouth, and a messy bedroom are diversions."

Lauren appreciated Dr. Cheaney's probing

questions. She hated the tendency of the other counselors to label Penny after hearing a five-minute summary of her history. Based on such a brief description, Penny could fit the criteria for many diagnoses but tagging her with a clinical syndrome didn't help root out her underlying distress.

"Those are good questions," Lauren replied. "Our initial treatment goals were straightforward. Penny wanted to get along better with her mother and make friends at school. But I agree that it's more than that."

"And no, Penny doesn't have needle tracks or evidence of self-injury," Lauren continued. "She's firm in her belief that her body is a temple, to be honored with good food and zero pollutants, like drugs or cigarettes. Her weight is normal, by the way."

Later, thinking that she would make a quick getaway after the clinical staff meeting, Lauren was surprised to see Kristen at her office door. "Do you have a minute?" Kristen asked hesitantly.

"Sure, Kristen. Come on in and shut the door. Anything wrong?"

"I didn't like how I sounded in the meeting and I wanted to say I'm sorry. You have the lowest no-show rate in the center but I was mouthing off about diagnoses. Obviously, you really know your clients and they do well. I get so frustrated with myself. Today I had three no-shows! I'm stuck."

Lauren smiled at Kristen, remembering her own early days as a social worker. There was so much to learn and most of the learning occurred in the trenches. "Do you want some feedback?" Lauren asked.

"Please. Don't spare me!" Kristen said, managing to look hopeful and anxious at the same time.

Lauren laughed. "I'm not going to bite. But without knowing much about your caseload, I do have some input on your style. For instance, is black your favorite color? You seem to wear a lot of it lately."

"No, it's my attempt to relate to my adolescent clients. My boyfriend said it would help them think I was more understanding, hipper. What do you think?" Kristen asked.

"I think our clients see through things like that," Lauren said gently, to reduce the sting of her words. "They know when we're being ourselves and when we're faking it. When Penny comes up with new slang or high school jargon, I just ask what she means. It puts her in control if only for a short minute. She'd know I was bluffing if I tried to figure it out through the back door."

Since Kristen seemed interested, Lauren continued. "Sometimes just being authentic works wonders. Penny chided me last session about my "old lady" sweater. I explained that our offices tend to run cold, so I keep the sweater in my drawer to use when I'm chilly. This led to her telling me about the time right after her parents' split, when she and her mom couched-surfed with assorted friends. Penny's memory of being cold in an impersonal space was triggered by my sweater and we did good grief work for the rest of the session."

"That's what I needed to hear," Kristen said. "If you had reacted badly to her insult about the sweater, she'd have continued the adolescent taunts. I'm so afraid to be myself. Ricky thinks I'm a moron and Dr. Cheaney says to be patient while I learn.

That's not extremely helpful when my clients don't show up. I can tell he's got other things on his mind, though."

"Yeah, mental health funding is always taking a hit and I think it wears on him," Lauren responded. "I've got other ideas for your therapeutic approach, if you want to hear them."

"Yes, please!"

"Well, you might want to think about what theory grounds your interventions with clients. I don't mean that you have to go all Sigmund Freud on them but I've found that having a theory to base my thinking on helps me feel more confident."

"So what theory do you like best?" Kristen asked.

"I'm not telling!" Lauren said, with a smile. "Seriously, though, what would you guess?"

"Maybe something that assumes people are basically good but that we all screw up at times," Kristen said. "That they can make things better, even if they've messed up. Is there a theory like that?"

"There are several. And your guess is right on the nose. For the record, Dr. Cheaney reminds me to be kind, but not stupid, and to challenge clients when they need it. Sometimes, I get overwhelmed with all the tragedy that we hear and frustrated when clients are stuck but my belief that people are trying their best helps me with those times."

Times like now, Lauren thought. Times when the future is murky. Times when Bryan and I can't agree what day of the week it is, much less about what we mean to each other.

After talking with Kristen, Lauren left for home. The staff meeting and the varied opinions about

Penny continued to bother her. Sometimes working with adolescents was like nailing pudding to a wall. They were too slippery to make firm contact.

Adding to her morose mood, she was aware that her symptoms of burnout were creeping back. Her recent contact with Doug, Jenny and Bill's wedding, and her uncertainty about Bryan's feelings had resulted in a blue mood most evenings after work. To top it all off, her meeting with Dr. Cheaney was scheduled for this week and he would be expecting an answer to his offer of the clinic director position.

Again, it was time to follow her own advice. She couldn't let her identity hinge on being with a man or on how much money she made. She would be fine if she were single for the rest of her life. And she could adopt a child or be a foster mom if she wanted children, which she did!

Once home, Lauren looked around her cozy surroundings. It was time for a new project. Painting appealed to her. It was an activity that allowed a person to cover all the old scratches and stains and start fresh. Now that her living room had pretty furniture, the dingy gray-green walls stood out.

Out with the old, in with the new, she vowed. My new mantra. Maybe I should make a cross stitch hanging with those words and put it over the sofa. Wonder where Bryan would fit? Is he old or new?

Two days later, Dr. Cheaney looked up from his computer, closing the test report he was writing. "These court evaluations are something, right Lauren?" he said. "I love forensic work but it's even more draining than our usual client load."

"I agree," Lauren replied. "That's why I stay away from custody and court issues. That line of work isn't my strength and I'm okay with that."

"Well, what's on your mind today?" Dr. Cheaney continued. "Anything new with Penny or her mom?"

"No, they come in tomorrow. I appreciated your comments at the clinical meeting. I need to figure out what Penny's after in therapy."

"Don't be too hard on yourself," Dr. Cheaney said. "Adolescents have special radar to sense our discomfort, so be patient. She'll let you know when she's ready or when she thinks her mom is ready."

"Good point," Lauren agreed. "While we're talking about letting someone know, I've made my decision about being clinic director. I'm truly honored by the offer but I can't take it. The work I love is therapy, not managing others and dealing with administrative hassles. And budgeting for anyone other than myself is my idea of pure torture. So thank you, but I can't accept."

"I completely understand, Lauren," Dr. Cheaney said. "After the clinical meeting, I could see your frustration with Kristen and Ricky. I could also tell that the thought of managing them was not what you wanted. So, what's your plan? Do you want to stay here and work for someone else? Or do you have other options?"

"For now, I'd like to stay. But my pipe dream, as it is for most clinicians, is to have a private practice eventually. Do you think that's crazy in this health insurance environment?"

"No, not crazy at all," Dr. Cheaney said with a

smile. "Collecting payments is a challenge but lots of people are making a go of it. Knowing you as I do, you'd have a thriving practice in no time."

The rest of the meeting was spent discussing other cases and Dr. Cheaney's plans for his move to the main office. He couldn't (or wouldn't) say who would be next in line for the director's position. Lauren hoped it wouldn't be Ricky. If so, Lauren's private practice would come sooner rather than later.

That evening, Lauren and Jenny met for supper. Jenny was full of honeymoon stories. Jenny described in detail the all-inclusive resort in Mexico, the wonderful food, and paddle boarding lessons with Bill. Rehashing the wedding and reception also consumed several minutes. Jenny's happiness was almost painful for Lauren but, at the same time, she was thrilled for her friend.

"So what's new with you?" Jenny asked. "Everything going well at the mental health center? How's the food pantry budget? Did you and Bryan get any wedding ideas from us?"

"Lots of questions!" Lauren teased back. She filled Jenny in on the uncertainty at the center, the possibilities for fund-raising for the pantry, and denied any wedding plans for herself and Bryan.

"I figured as much," Jenny said. "You two were looking very romantic as you danced at the reception but then you avoided him until Bill and I left for the hotel. What happened this time?"

Lauren's eyes narrowed. "This time, as with all the other times, Bryan's focus was on my steady income, probably because he may not have one of his own soon. I'm so done with men counting on me to pay the bills!"

Jenny looked at her friend in disbelief. "You can't be serious. Bryan's not like Doug and I'm convinced that's what you're thinking. Bryan would never rely on you to shoulder the bills. You know better, Lauren."

"I guess I do know better but, in the moment, his comment struck me as being about him, not me. He said a regular income means a lot these days, as if I didn't get that, after all we went through when my dad was unemployed. No, Jenny, he was talking about his own fear of the future not my decision to risk a private practice." Lauren angrily speared a lettuce leaf, causing a crouton to bounce to the floor.

The supper ended in tense small talk. Lauren drove home in a funk. Was she really misinterpreting Bryan's comment? Would her father's history, and Doug's betrayal, always color how she expected men to behave when life got difficult? Why couldn't she get past all of that and focus on her own goals?

Chapter Twelve

The first month of the New Year meant long lines again at the food pantry. Most clients were patient but the atmosphere was decidedly flat when compared to the excitement from a few weeks ago. The post-holiday blues had descended on the clientele. In fact, most of the volunteers looked a little grim.

"It's so quiet!" Sally commented when she had a break from loading frozen chicken thighs into client order boxes. "What's going on?"

Lauren smiled at Sally's appearance. Gone was the fashionable matron. In her place, stood a woman wearing jeans and a ratty sweatshirt. The shirt, once a high-end designer piece, was stained with chicken drippings.

"It's the same for all of us, probably," Lauren replied. "Christmas is over and the hope the season brought is now replaced by our regular daily challenges. Yesterday when we got all the snow, my dad said if it were a month earlier, we'd have been excited. Now we're just irritated and hope our commute to work isn't too badly affected."

"I guess so," Sally said. "Could we play some music to lighten the mood?"

"We've tried that in the past, but there were always arguments about the songs we picked. So we just let it go."

"Let me deal with this," Sally said.

She marched to the auditorium and announced, "It's too solemn in here. I've got a playlist on my phone that mixes every musical genre around. Who's willing to give it a try? It's only fair to listen to at least five songs before you judge. Hopefully, by then, you'll have your order filled and be out of here."

People laughed and agreed to give the new volunteer's selections a fair shake. Lauren was amazed at Sally's solution and at her playlist. It included everything from Adele to Frank Sinatra, from Bruno Mars to Josh Grobin, and beyond.

"Nicely done!" Lauren laughed. "Sally, you are a woman of many layers. I love your playlist. Send it to me, please!"

After the pantry closed, Lauren skipped the usual lunch with Jenny to work on the three inches of snow in her driveway. Her father was right. If this were the Saturday before Christmas, she would be awash with holiday cheer. Now, shoveling was just another chore and a cold one at that.

As she wiped her dripping nose, she noticed Bryan driving by. His car stopped, his automatic trunk opened, and he retrieved a snow shovel. Great.

"Need some help?" he asked.

"What are you doing in this neighborhood?" Lauren asked tersely.

"That's not a very gracious response to a generous offer," Bryan said calmly. "I was on my way to the grocery and thought I'd see if you were home. Other than help shoveling your driveway, is there anything you need?"

"Nope, I've got plenty of food," she answered. "And the driveway is almost clear, as you can see."

"What about your sidewalks? Need any help with them?" Bryan eyed the long walk leading to Lauren's front porch.

"No, it will all melt soon, according to the weather report," Lauren said. "There's no HOA in this old neighborhood to complain to me about the walks. I just wanted to be sure I didn't get stuck in the driveway before work on Monday."

Lauren knew she was being petty but she ignored the prick of her conscience. Why did this man bug her so much? Didn't he have anything better to do on a winter Saturday than bother her with sweet offers to shovel her walk?

Bryan admitted defeat. "Fine, then," he said. "Enjoy the rest of your weekend."

As he drove away, Bryan assessed Lauren's appearance. Her old snow boots had pom-pom tassels and she was wearing those tight jeans he liked. Her large parka and snug knitted cap completed the usual Lauren look, eclectic and unintentionally appealing. As he pulled away, he looked in his rearview mirror as she began to shovel her sidewalks. He'd known that she would be responsible, clearing them so no one would fall. She, obviously, didn't want him to be the one to do it though.

On Monday, Penny and her mother, Sheila, entered Lauren's office in glum silence. Lauren greeted them and after exchanging catch-up stories about their holiday celebrations, she suggested that they begin with whatever concerns they were most anxious about.

Sheila began. "Thank you for all you've done for Penny, Lauren. Despite our differences, we're getting along a little better in the last few weeks. But I still think Penny's hiding something from me. When I ask directly, she clams up, puts in her ear buds, and heads to her room."

"Can't I just have some privacy?" the girl exclaimed, tossing her purple hair, which was now sporting light brown roots, to one side. "It would be abnormal to tell your mom everything, right, Lauren?"

The hairs on Lauren's neck bristled, which was usually a sign something was wrong. Her clinical radar rarely failed her.

"You're right about needing privacy," she said to Penny. "But I'm getting the feeling that this is more than that. There's a secret here. Secrets can be wonderful, even powerful. They can also be dangerous or scary. I think that's why your mom may be hovering more than usual."

"Exactly, Lauren," Sheila agreed. "I know I can overwhelm Penny with my questions, especially since her father left. I'm probably relying on her too much for companionship. I get why you would resent that, Penny. But in the past you'd laugh and tell me to butt out. Now you close down completely."

Penny gave Lauren a hard stare and replied to her mother. "No one's closing down, Mom. I want to be with my friends, that's all. You don't need to know everything we talk about. You and your new boyfriend need to get lives of your own."

The session evolved into mild chaos after that. Penny aired grievances about Sheila's choice of men since her father had left the marriage. Sheila was angry about Penny's appearance, slovenly habits, and attitude. As Lauren listened, she became more sure Penny's tirade was a cover with Sheila buying in to the girl's diversionary tactics.

Lauren broke in. "Enough of this for now," she said evenly. "You two might as well be reading from a script because I can predict what you'll say before you say it. What's really going on?"

Penny and Sheila sat without responding. Lauren continued. "Okay, Sheila, as you look at Penny, what's the first feeling that comes to you?"

"I'm afraid for her," Sheila said as her eyes misted. "My instincts tell me she's in danger."

Lauren expected the usual dramatic eye roll and sigh from Penny but didn't get them. Penny stared at her mother.

"Danger? What's dangerous about meeting new people? This dead-end town is full of losers. My friends and I have been talking online to people in Indy, so what?"

Penny's words hung in the air. Lauren knew she had to be careful or Penny would shut down again. "What do you guys talk about?" Lauren asked innocently, forcing herself not to immediately jump to specific questions about sexting, and more.

"Just the usual," Penny said. "School, friends, where we'd like to go to college. The guys from Indianapolis are way more sophisticated than the dweebs from Gordon. They have real goals. A couple of them have already started their own businesses online and they're making real money."

With that, Lauren knew Penny could be courting serious trouble. It could be nothing but, on the other hand, human trafficking was rampant in the Midwest. Perpetrators often preyed on young girls via innocent meetings online, eventually arranging to connect in person. Often, they used the lure of affluence, especially with victims whose families were struggling. The grooming could go on for months or girls could be taken against their will at the first face-to-face contact. Again, Lauren had to be careful.

"That's impressive. What kind of businesses?" Lauren asked. "These fellows sound sharp."

"Not sure," Penny hedged. "It's complicated, something about virus protection services, I think."

Sheila looked increasingly worried. "What do you know about these guys, Penny? They could be fifty-years-old for all you know. You never can tell who you're talking to online."

"Thanks for being utterly predictable, Mom," Penny said sarcastically. "You always jump to the most paranoid conclusions possible. I can tell who's fifty and these guys sound nothing like you."

Lauren broke in before Sheila could respond that she was only forty. "So they're smart, savvy guys. When are you going to meet?"

"How'd you know we were going to get together?" Penny asked, horrified. "Mom, have you been looking at my phone?"

"No, but maybe I should have," Sheila sputtered. "You are not meeting anyone without me being there."

"Seems reasonable," Lauren said. "Penny, you've told me you were glad your mom met her dates for the first time in a restaurant, with her friends watching a few tables over. You didn't want her to be threatened, or worse, by a stranger."

"It's not the same at all," Penny shouted. "Mom was on a dating site. She had no idea who she was going to meet. These guys talk about their classes, who won the basketball game last week, blah, blah. They're legit."

"Maybe," Lauren said. "Or maybe they watch the news for the high school scores. They can tell you about what uniforms the cheerleaders wore, how the last second shot made all the difference, and on and on. There's no way to know, is there Penny?"

"How can we be sure you're safe?" Sheila asked. "Would you and your friends be willing for me and their moms to be around when you all get together?"

Lauren was pleased that Sheila had focused on Penny's wellbeing instead of blaming her for keeping secrets. Penny, however, was not pleased.

"Are you kidding, Mom?" she asked. "Like my buds are going to have their moms around when we finally meet these great guys?"

"What about you, Penny? Would you be willing to have your mom play back-up, just in case?" Lauren was counting on Penny's sense of self-preservation, which to date had been good, based on her concerns about her mother's dating life.

"Maybe," Penny said slowly. "I'll think about it."

The session ended with Lauren praising the hard work Penny and Sheila had done. An appointment was set for next week and, in the meantime, Penny promised her mother no meeting with the Indy guys would be set for the weekend.

Lauren realized that Dr. Cheaney had been right. Penny wanted to tell her secret because she was scared to keep it but she had to be sure her mom would hear it without exploding or grounding her. Lauren also knew Penny was excruciatingly lonely, missing her dad, and longing for a relationship with her mother on a more equal footing.

One thing at a time, Lauren thought. We're peeling the therapeutic onion. Penny's onion has several layers to get through but, in the process, we have to keep her safe.

Lauren continued to think about the session that evening at home. As she microwaved her dinner, she wondered if she was making too much of the possible hazard Penny's online friends could pose. Was she turning into a fear-based person with no faith in others? Better to be cautious, though. Penny was a sharp kid but her judgment was iffy and that was putting a positive spin on it.

January and February were typically slow months in the retail world but Bryan was solemn as he looked at Mohr's numbers for the first two weeks of the year. They were dismal, to say the least. At this rate, the store would need to close by April. The news of other retailers wasn't encouraging either. Sears, Macy's, and even some of the big box stores were regularly in the headlines as their financial woes were detailed.

What now? It was time for an action plan. The management team had to do something to save the store. It was time to go big or go home. He sounded like his father. Clichés came easy when they were stumped.

As with previous online searches, his research began with a study of successful brick-and-mortar businesses. One idea suddenly struck him as being potentially helpful to Mohr's. It involved scaling back merchandise offered at the existing store and incorporating a strong online business presence of those remaining selections. Since Mohr's strength was in women's apparel, it made sense to focus on that area when limiting inventory. Special occasion clothing, including wedding gowns and veils, was a high profit-margin category, so that area would be promoted heavily. Maybe Mathas' coupons could be helpful to the process of Mohr's rebranding. A coupon could offer a discount on dresses costing over a certain price point, with a free lunch entrée at the tearoom or whatever idea made financial sense to move merchandise.

Bryan continued his work online, looking for other ideas to bolster Mohr's sales. He read an interview with a college business professor. "'The future of traditional retail may lie in experiential sales. For example, toy stores, where children craft their own doll or stuffed animal to take home, use hands-on experiences as a way to increase sales. Home improvement and fabric stores offer weekly classes to build customer skills and improve revenue. Customers can't get enough of it.'"

Bryan absorbed the information and he realized Mohr's couture wedding line should include more than just trying on dresses. Lauren had said making Jenny's veil was easy. Maybe veil kits could be sold in the store as well as online. Brides, their friends, and family members could make a veil to match the dress they chose. But how would brides with no crafting experience be part of the concept? How would that work?

"'The average wedding in the US costs between twenty- and thirty-thousand dollars,'" he read, as he scrolled through page after page of online information. "'And in addition to the price of wedding gowns, costs for veils can reach several hundred dollars.'"

Bryan shook his head, shocked at the cost of something made of such flimsy materials. He looked at bargain veil sites, discovering discount prices. His experienced eye, though, could tell that the veils were made of synthetic materials and low-quality lace. Threads were left untrimmed and beading was glued on randomly. Maybe there was a real market for veil kits. Homemade had to be better than what he was seeing on these sites.

His creative juices began to flow. If Mohr's could establish a reputation as a destination for high-quality women's clothing, with an emphasis on wedding attire, they could also build an Internet store that included customized, do-it-yourself wedding veils in addition to the clothing offered in the store. The kits would not be difficult for Mohr's to assemble, or subcontract, if the choices of veil length, lace, and tulle color were limited to three or four each. Pricing the kits at just under a hundred dollars or so would allow good profit, while at the same time allowing customers to take pride in creating an heirloom veil made of natural materials.

The marketing folks could sell this idea in an

instant, linking the Mohr's brand to timeless wedding and special occasion dresses. Bryan closed his laptop with a thud. He needed to bounce these ideas off someone to be sure they were feasible. His father would scoff, he knew. Tom Dawson was not a crafty type and would likely see Bryan's plans as diminishing the image of the store Tom helped create.

As he had so often in recent months, Bryan wished he could run his ideas by Lauren. Her expertise in sewing and bridal fashion was not the reason, though. He missed Lauren's enthusiasm, encouragement, and her belief that Mohr's was worth saving. He missed being able to brainstorm ideas with someone he trusted. He also missed her touch and the feel of her lips on his. She was perfect for him, he realized, but, for whatever reason, she distanced herself from him each time he thought they were finally getting close.

After Lauren finished her meal, her thoughts went back to Bryan's comment at the wedding reception. What's wrong with me? she thought. He was trying to be helpful when I was discussing the risks of private practice. But I immediately assumed he wanted to lean on me financially.

As she reflected on these familiar themes, she became angry, this time at herself. Okay, so my father went through a couple of jobless years when my mother had to be the sole breadwinner. Doug couldn't keep a job and I had to help with his bills. Life happens and Mohr's might close but it doesn't mean that Bryan would use me for money.

The weekend brought a welcome respite from the stress of the clinic. Lines at the food pantry were long but patrons were patient, due in part to Sally's new music mix. Several clients commented, however, that the food packs were smaller than last year's. Lauren had posted signs explaining inventory was low but that steps were in place to improve quantities and food selection.

At lunch, after the pantry closed, Jenny, Sally, and Lauren discussed the progress of the food pantry cookbook fundraiser. "We've got twenty pantry clients who have offered recipes so far," Jenny commented. "They sound delicious and I'm making one of them tonight for Bill. It's a casserole that uses pasta, canned chicken, and Misty's herb mix, with a base of canned cream soup. I think Sally's trainer has added the perfect touch to our cookbook with her seasoning blend."

"One of my so-called friends used to say she refused to make recipes that called for canned soup," Sally said, arching her brow. "Of course, she refused to cook at all! She ate salads twice a day and her husband relied on deli meat sandwiches for most of his dinners at home."

"Yes, those soups contain artificial ingredients and preservatives but they're a good alternative to going hungry. They also help stretch the protein in the meal," Lauren said. "Maybe we could also include a recipe for homemade cream soup mix. I remember seeing one that was based on powdered milk. And since we have trouble getting rid of the powdered milk in the food packs, that would be the perfect use for it."

"Based on other fundraising cookbooks, I'm estimating we'll need several hundred recipes," Sally said. "We have a way to go, even with cream soup mix added to the tally."

"Recipes can be submitted by anyone, right?" Jenny asked. "As long as they use products provided by the pantry?"

"Right," Lauren said. "I've made a master list of those items. We can distribute it to people we know who are good cooks and see what happens. If you think about the number of recipes a person cooks over the course of a year, it shouldn't be too difficult for our friends to come up with the number we need."

Sally's pressure on her contacts in the fundraising world had resulted in a cookbook publisher willing to discount the usual fees in return for acknowledgment on the title page. Once recipes were collected, the publisher promised a two-month turn around, with delivery of the books in time for the harvest of Indiana garden tomatoes and other homegrown goodies. Misty had delivered the first two hundred herb packets, ready for attachment to the front inside cover of the book.

"We're on a roll, ladies," Sally gushed. "When we have the books in hand, I guarantee we'll sell at least a thousand copies, many of them to my friends who owe me favors. At ten dollars profit per book, the food pantry will be on solid footing again for several months. And our publisher also suggested online copies to keep sales continuous for even longer."

"That's great," Jenny said. "What about other services? Could we provide more, now that we're running in the black? What about Lauren's idea of special occasion kid's clothing?"

"I agree, Jenny," Sally said. "There are services in place for job seekers – interview practice, professional clothing, and so on. But no one offers special clothing for children. How could we get that going?"

Several options were discussed, with Sally more than willing to sound out her friends about making girl's dresses and boy's vests with matching bow ties.

"My friends are a talented bunch," Sally said. "We could gradually build an inventory of clothing and allow pantry clients to choose one outfit per year, per quarter, per month. The frequency of our offerings will depend on whatever amount of clothing we can keep in stock."

That afternoon, Lauren was busy vacuuming her living room when the phone rang. She saw that it was Bryan and answered the call with caution. "Are you okay, Bryan?" she asked. "It's a surprise to hear from you."

"I'm fine but I need to talk," Bryan blurted. "I apologize in advance if you think I'm using you. But I've got ideas for Mohr's future rattling around in my head and I need a sounding board. Like it or not, your opinion means more to me than anyone else's."

Silence greeted Bryan's outburst. Lauren finally replied. "My opinion matters more than anyone's?" she asked softly. "That's a real compliment, Bryan. While we're apologizing, it's my turn now. You were just trying to help me at the reception when you talked about the importance of a job with a salary. My fear got in the way, as usual, and I'm sorry. I'll be over in a half hour."

Lauren arrived with chicken salad sandwiches and fruit, having been alerted by Bryan that he needed to talk through his ideas at length. After a two-hour discourse, with Lauren asking a few pertinent questions, he exhaled slowly.

"So what do you think?" he asked. "Could Mohr's pare down to a high-end women's clothing destination and incorporate a designer wedding line, complete with veil kits?"

"Wow, I think it could," Lauren said. "You mentioned the need for helpers for the veil-making idea, which dovetails with an idea we've been thinking about for the food pantry."

Lauren explained the goal of providing dressy clothing for the children of pantry clients and Sally's suggestions that 4-H members or women's clubs could help with the effort.

Lauren continued. "If Mohr's could provide materials and notions at cost, along with space for sewing machines and assembly, both the retail and charity goals could be successful. It would also be good public relations to combine the two."

Bryan smiled at Lauren. "I haven't felt this hopeful in a long time. Thanks for the food and for listening. It means so much to me. No, you mean so much to me."

He leaned across the small dining nook table and kissed her. What began as a casual kiss of gratitude deepened until both of them broke away, each short of breath.

"You mean a lot to me, too," Lauren said. "Your devotion to Mohr's and to your family, is really sexy."

"What?" Bryan laughed. "How does my concern about my family and business translate to sexy? Not that I'm arguing."

"You care so much for others, you're loyal, and you fight for what's right. Even when the odds are terrible. To use cookbook jargon, those are the ingredients of a wonderful man," Lauren said.

"They make for a wonderful woman, too," Bryan replied. "Everything you said applies to you also."

At that moment, each of their phones jingled with incoming text messages. Jenny's message to Lauren, and Bill's to Bryan, were identical and cryptic. "Care for some dessert?"

"Are they spying on us?" Bryan asked in frustration. His doorbell rang and the newly married couple appeared. Bill carried a bakery box full of treats.

"We wanted to see our favorite wedding party members. When you weren't home, Lauren, we crossed our fingers that you'd be here with Bryan," Jenny teased. "It's a great night for cuddling by the fire, right?"

Lauren blushed. Bryan gritted his teeth. The foursome enjoyed dessert together, while Jenny and Bill reported on their honeymoon in Cozumel. Jenny's wit made their stories hilarious, especially when she described their afternoon of deep-sea fishing. The waves were rough and as Jenny put it, "We fed the fish for sure, but not with bait! We were both green when we got back to shore!"

As Bill and Jenny drove home, Jenny speculated about Lauren and Bryan. "We definitely interrupted something. But Lauren is so wounded. I wonder if she'll ever really open up to Bryan."

"Bryan's no easy case either," Bill said dryly. "Angela did a number on him. He entered the MBA program full of confidence but when he came home he was consumed with doubt. I met her once. She was very cold but a real looker. Nothing like you, honey."

"Thanks so much, honey," Jenny retorted, as they both laughed. "I know what you meant, though. After Lauren found out about Doug sleeping with his boss, she was devastated. She's smart and beautiful but I think she still believes no man will ever love her."

"What a pair," Bill said. "How can we help them?"

"I'm not sure," Jenny said. "If being in the most romantic wedding in the state of Indiana didn't do it, what will? Despite my history of meddling, I think we should let them figure it out."

Bill glanced at Jenny. "You're right, as usual. I knew there was a reason I married you."

Jenny scooted over next to Bill on the old sedan's bench seat. "This ancient beater is nothing to look at but I like riding next to you. Very romantic."

Lauren left Bryan's apartment soon after Jenny and Bill, saying she had to get up early the next day for church. At home, she thought about her usual prayer request list: family, friends, and health. She added a fervent prayer of gratitude that she and

Bryan were becoming closer with what seemed to be a new level of honesty between them. She also added a prayer for Bryan and his quest to save Mohr's.

He's on to something, dear Lord. Please give him wisdom, perseverance, and lots of luck through it all.

Chapter Thirteen

Bryan invited himself to his parents' home for Sunday supper. He also asked if Bill, Jenny, and Bill's parents could attend. After pleasantries were exchanged, Bryan began his business pitch, one worthy of his capstone MBA course.

He detailed his online research summarizing current problems and possible solutions to the many woes of traditional retailers. His plan to focus on high-end dresses and formal bridal wear, along with online sales and veil kits, was described with confidence and enthusiasm. When he finished, he looked at the six shocked faces and waited for their response.

"It's a lot to absorb," he said, breaking the long silence. "But we all know Mohr's is breathing its last. The consultants, who made a small fortune from us, gave no hope except liquidation and splitting the spoils. They ignored Mohr's value to Gordon, to the community, and to its employees. I'm convinced we can do better."

Tom spoke first. "You're right, son. It is a lot to

take in. I'm no expert on this online approach but I'm intrigued."

Bill's father, Dean, spoke up. "I agree with Tom. I've got questions, though. What will we do with the two upper floors of Mohr's? Based on your plan, we would only need the main floor and the adjoining tearoom. And what about our staff? I hate the thought of layoffs but I guess there's no way around that."

"Layoffs, early retirements, retraining staff. All those are likely possibilities. But they're better than total liquidation," Bryan said. "I also agree that Mohr's upper floors will need to be repurposed. I think those two floors would make great apartments. Small towns all over the country are revitalizing their downtown areas and they always begin with housing in the middle of the action."

"Or they could be condos, not apartments," Sally chimed in. "Tom, we could buy one. After all, we've been thinking about selling the lake house."

Mavis was aghast. "Sally, you can't be serious. You love that house. Do you want to share walls with strangers at this stage of your life?"

Sally laughed. "Sis, this stage of my life is full of surprises. I've already put out some feelers with a realtor friend about listing the lake house. She said there are several pro athletes in Indianapolis looking for a secluded retreat that's still an easy drive back to the city."

Sally continued with other ideas. "Another possibility is to use some of the space for offices, leased to Gordon small business owners. Maybe Lauren will want to rent from us if she goes into private practice. The anonymity of going into a multi-function building would be appealing to her clients."

Bryan looked at his mother in wonder. She was, clearly, working an agenda but he loved her for it. If only Lauren would agree and believe that she wasn't being manipulated, instead, being offered a leg up on the private practice challenge.

Supper, cooked entirely by Sally, proceeded. Despite the intensity of the conversation, everyone (except perhaps Mavis) had a sense of hopeful relief. Tom, Bryan, Bill, and Dean spent another two hours talking about Bryan's plan, hammering out first steps, timelines, and possible hiccups. Tom made plans to call Mohr's lawyer in the morning to set the process in motion. Bryan's task was to contact their banker for financing to get the company through the time of corporate restructuring, remodeling, and severance payments to those choosing early retirement.

The meeting at the bank was not the smooth sailing Bryan had anticipated. Jack Feherty, Mohr's business banker for almost twenty years, was cool to Bryan's proposal to save the store.

"Have you thought this through?" Jack asked. "At first glance, liquidation seems your best bet. I believe that's the option in the best interest of your family. You could all come out with a sizeable cash settlement given the conservative way you've managed Mohr's over the years. And my sources around town have said your consultants recommended liquidation as well."

So much for professional confidentiality, Bryan

thought. "Consultant" is a kind word for people like that.

"But we don't want to liquidate," Bryan said, his jaw set. "The store is viable. We need a niche market, which we've discovered with the combination of women's clothing and wedding attire. Adding to those is our online presence with the option for brides on a budget to order veil kits. We'll be able to serve customers at different income levels which will further enhance our appeal in the future."

"Your condo and office idea makes the plan better but I'd still need to see what you're talking about in terms of those kits," Jack said. "You can't expect funding like this without the bank seeing what we're investing in. We don't want to be stuck with middle school home ec projects if you fold. There's no resale value for us in unfinished veils. We need to protect our investment."

Bryan stayed cool, in spite of his urge to walk out on Jack. "I understand completely," he said. "Do you have any time next week for a presentation on the kits?"

As he left, Bryan wondered what he'd committed to. Could his mother find some crafty friends to develop professional-looking veil kits by next week? He could ask Lauren but she might be miffed and assume he was trying to take advantage of her for the store's sake. After remembering their positive interaction on Saturday night, (interrupted by Bill and Jenny, unfortunately), he decided it was worth the risk.

Bryan called and left a message since Lauren was in session. "Here's the deal, Lauren. I'm in a bind and I need help with the veil kits by next week or the bank won't lend us the money to salvage the store. Truth be told, I guess I am using you for your expertise but I'm willing to pay you a consulting fee. Let me know what you think."

Lauren called Bryan after work, feeling both surprised and pleased that he needed her. "No, pal, I'm not going to charge you a consulting fee," she bantered. "Let's talk, and we can brainstorm what you need."

Bryan sighed with relief. She hadn't refused but he sensed that she was tentative about helping him. "I think we should have at least three, preferably four, veil kits to demo for Jack. That would mean four unfinished kits with all the supplies clearly labeled and with instructions for every step of the creation process. Then, we'd need four partially finished veils so Jack could see what the actual process involves. Lastly, we'd need four finished veils. Ideally, we should purchase some veils from a bridal shop in Indianapolis so that Jack can compare our veils with theirs and hopefully, see that ours are as good or better than what people spend several hundreds of dollars for."

"Sure, that's easy," Lauren said sarcastically. "And you want all that in under a week?"

"I know, I know," Bryan said. "I had to be smooth in the moment or Jack would have seen the deer-in-the-headlights look I've had so often lately."

Lauren laughed. "Okay, you've sold me. We can do this, Dawson. And I owe your mother for all her work in saving the food pantry. We're on track for full funding for the rest of the year, thanks to her cookbook idea. I'll go to the fabric store after work on Friday and buy what we need."

Bryan ended the call with mixed emotions. Lauren was full of teasing good humor but said she owed his mother. Was she helping out just to repay Sally for her work at the food pantry? And she'd called him pal. Surely they were more than pals!

Saturday was set as Veil Kit Production Day. Sally, Jenny, Janice, and Mavis were recruited to work an assembly line for the twelve veils, four each in various stages of production. Lauren, Mavis, and Janice had sewing experience so Sally and Jenny were in charge of assembling the unfinished kits and creating instructional materials. Bryan and Tom drove to Indianapolis to purchase the retail veils. They had orders to buy four different veils, covering a range of prices.

Jenny used her contacts at the high school so they were free to use the sewing room for their work. Lauren, as usual, had each step organized so the teams could work efficiently. After three hours of labor, four completed veils were produced. In addition, the three seamstresses wore bandages, having stuck themselves numerous times as they hurried to do the hand-stitching required to finish the veils.

"These look wonderful," Sally gushed. "Mavis, I've always been awestruck by your sewing talent. I can't wait to compare these with the veils the men buy."

"They do look good, despite my having to dab bleach on that one blood stain," Mavis said.

The two sets of unfinished veil kits, (one completely unfinished and one partially completed), were compiled quickly. Each woman was anxious about how to price the kits.

"We know what we've spent for the raw materials," Jenny said. "The final pricing will depend on how our creations stack up with the veils from the shop in Indianapolis. I think our veils are going to be very comparable but I want to see the retail product first."

Mavis agreed and added, "I think another factor is how much our costs at the wholesale level will be. Lauren bought all these materials at retail price because we were in a hurry."

Bryan and Tom entered the sewing lab at that moment. Pulling out the veils they'd purchased, they discussed the unforeseen challenges of the afternoon.

"The salespeople at the bridal shop didn't know what to make of us," Tom said dryly. "They weren't sure if we were buying for ourselves, for a costume event, or as secret shoppers for their competition. We left them wondering!"

Lauren had another thought. "I think we should buy a few discounted veils online," she said. "I did some research and, sometimes, the quality is awful. Several reviewers complained about loose threads, glue smears, and pearls that fell off mid-ceremony. Bryan should show Jack the cheap veils, in addition to the expensive retail samples, so that he can see how wonderful our veils are. We can use rush delivery for the bargain veils if we need to."

"Are you sure you've chosen the right profession?" Tom asked Lauren. "That's a terrific idea. We'll show Jack our competition at both ends of the spectrum. Lauren, I think there's a budding businesswoman inside you."

Bryan smiled as his father praised Lauren. She was a constant surprise. Just when he was sure she was a buttoned-up, by-the-books type, she came up with unexpected insights. He wondered if he would ever know the real Lauren. He was also secretly pleased at her use of the phrase "our veils" as she talked to his father. Maybe she was warming up to the Dawson clan and to him.

Another hour was spent comparing the handmade veils with those from Indy. Lauren's experienced eye noted subtle differences that would make their final product even more competitive. Bryan's eyes darkened as he looked at her. She was all concentration, trying on the longest veil. Her petite frame was enveloped in the cathedral-length creation as she looked at her reflection in the sewing room mirror, rotating slowly so that she could see the veil from all angles.

"Looks good on you," he said solemnly. "Maybe you could model for the online ads."

"Not likely," Lauren responded. "You need a professional which will add to your costs. Hope you budgeted that in when you talked to Jack."

Tom chimed in. "That's what I'm talking about," he said. "Bryan, we've got to get this girl out of mental health. We need her talents for the business."

"Not likely," Lauren chuckled. "I have enough stress with my own bottom line to worry about anyone else's."

Bryan noticed that Lauren hadn't bristled at his father's mention of using her business savvy to help Mohr's. How could she be so accepting of his father's praise? If Bryan had said the same thing, she'd have invented a reason to leave.

At home assembling leftovers to reheat, Lauren replayed the events of the day. Despite the unspoken pressure experienced by the Dawson clan, everyone had worked together well. She was impressed that Bryan's devotion to saving Mohr's was shared equally by his family. Tom's praise of her business acumen was also a shock. She reveled in his enthusiasm, secretly pleased that she could be of use in areas other than choosing fabric and trim. What would it be like to be a part of such a tight-knit family? Her family was close but it included only three people since Aunt Abby's death. Her parents loved her without question and, for that, she was forever grateful. It would be fun, though, to be a member of a larger family.

And what had Bryan meant when he'd said that the veil looked good on her? Was he teasing or hinting at a future for the two of them? She was afraid to hope for a commitment from him but she admitted she was doing exactly that. What would it be like to be married to Bryan? She didn't need to wonder. She knew it would be wonderful.

At their appointment the next week, Penny and Sheila entered Lauren's office with looks of trepidation. Lauren had expected conflict but their demeanors seemed different. Neither was angry but both were tense.

"Tell her," Sheila said. "Lauren needs to know what happened this weekend."

"Mom, it's not that big of a deal," Penny replied. "Lauren, we were all online talking to the guys in

Indy, as usual, and now we're going to meet. Before you say anything, YES, we're meeting in public, and YES, Mom will be at the restaurant."

"That's a good plan, Penny. You and your mom are looking like a team again. But, nosy woman that I am, I want to know how it all came about," Lauren said.

Sheila nodded, almost imperceptibly. She was obviously concerned about the upcoming meeting.

"Well, Bobby – he's a senior at a school on the north side of Indianapolis – suggested we meet at a middle distance between Indy and Gordon. They don't have any basketball games next weekend so the timing is perfect. We're going to the Burger Hut on I70 just south of Greencastle," Penny enthused, twirling her hair.

"How will you all connect? What do these guys look like? I assume you've seen pictures of them? Any video chats?" Lauren tried to pace her questions, being careful not to reveal her own anxiety.

"We've seen pics and yeah, they're both hot. My friend Tracy is coming with me. The other moms weren't cool with it, though. Mom, you've really come through for us."

Sheila sighed. "I'm not cool with it either, sweetie. I just know you well enough that you'll sneak out if I forbid you to go to the meeting. I need to protect you somehow. You know nothing about these guys."

"So now I know nothing!" Penny exclaimed. "Just when I thought we were getting close again."

"Your mom didn't say that," Lauren said firmly. "She said you know nothing about these guys. Bobby and whoever."

"And honestly," Lauren continued, "your mom is being way cooler than nine out of ten moms I know. If there are good guys to meet, she wants you to meet them. If not, she wants to be there for you and Tracy."

Penny grudgingly agreed. "I get that," she said. "Anyway, this weekend is looking up for a change. My big plans usually include a rented movie and frozen pizza at Tracy's house."

When the session was over, Lauren had a rare two-hour block of time, allocated on her schedule for writing reports and reviewing intern notes. Instead, she put in a call to Dr. Cheaney. His experience with forensic cases was just what she needed, either to allay her fears for Penny or to plan a course of action to keep the young girl safe.

"Hi Dr. Cheaney, it's Lauren. I need to run a situation by you that's got me worried." Lauren described Penny's online interactions with the boys from Indianapolis, including the plan, suggested by the "hot guys" to meet at the Burger Hut on the interstate.

"What do you think, Dr. Cheaney? Am I making too much of this?" she asked.

"It's unusual Penny has never had a live chat with Bobby. Didn't they interact with Skype or Face-Time? And it's interesting the boys suggested Burger Hut," he replied slowly. "Often predators avoid the major food chains on the highway since chain restaurants have more traffic and better-trained management. Often, they have paid guards and security cameras, too. The smaller restaurants tend to be understaffed and lack cameras. They have quieter parking lots which makes changing cars and a quick getaway easier."

Goosebumps spread over Lauren's body as she listened to Dr. Cheaney. "What should I do? I know one of the owners of the Burger Hut. Should I tell him?"

"Let me call one of my contacts at the State Police," he said. "They work closely with the feds and deal with abductions all the time. They'll give us some good input."

Paperwork consumed the rest of the day although Lauren had to force herself to concentrate. Unwilling to wait for Dr. Cheaney's call, she decided to phone Bryan to get his input. She wouldn't break confidentiality but as a partial owner of Burger Hut, he had a right to know of the potential police action on Saturday.

Her call was met with an enthusiastic "How's my favorite social worker?" when Bryan answered. After they had bantered for a few minutes, Lauren asked if he was free for dinner.

"Once again, we're thinking in sync," he said. "I've been wanting to thank you one more time for all the help with the veil kits. My family has new hope for the business, in large part due to your expertise."

"You're welcome but no thanks are needed. I had fun with your family. But I have to talk to you about something else," Lauren said anxiously. "Nothing's wrong with me, or us, but I need your feedback on a development at work."

Since neither of them wanted to meet in public, Bryan offered to host at his apartment. "What's your pleasure? Ordering in is a major skill of mine. Pizza, subs, food truck?"

"I'm glad I'm dating a man with skills," Lauren said. "How about the new barbecue food truck, with the gourmet frosted cupcakes for dessert?"

"Wow, you're either hungry or tense," Bryan responded. "Or both."

"Both," she said.

After dinner had been polished off, they sat and discussed the latest developments in their lives. Lauren insisted that Bryan share his day first. He detailed the lengthy family discussion after the veil assembly marathon and said that he, his father, and the Sturms had made significant progress in developing a plan to roll out the new version of Mohr's.

"We should be operating in our new format by mid-year. As you know, we'll focus on women's boutique and special occasion clothing, with veil kits to accompany bridal wear," he said proudly. "We've also hired a website consultant to help with the online push, along with a logistics expert."

"And my meeting today with Jack went much better than the first one but we did have a rocky start," he continued. "The veil kits, along with the samples from Indy, really confused him at first. He said they all looked alike. He couldn't tell one cloud of white from another. Jack was almost ready to close the meeting but I insisted he owed me the hour he'd scheduled. I had the inexpensive online veils delivered overnight and I spent twenty minutes showing him their defects. Then I compared our quality work to theirs. Those cheap veils were the icing on the wedding cake, so to speak. Jack couldn't believe the poor-quality workmanship.

They made our handmade veils look even better." Bryan took a breath and went on as if he were afraid the pause would undo the effects of the successful pitch.

"Then, once he saw the veils going for hundreds of dollars, he had to admit ours were as good or even better. He said he'd personally vouch to the board for approving the loan to Mohr's. It's exciting but frightening, all at once." Despite his words, Bryan looked more relaxed than Lauren had seen him in several months.

"Well, regardless of all the work and uncertainty, you look like you're having the time of your life," she smiled. "I'm happy for you and your family."

"But what's your news?" Bryan asked. "You don't look relaxed at all."

"Good observation, Dawson. I swear, you could be a therapist if you put your mind to it," she said with a frown. "I need to tell you about a situation at work that may involve the Burger Hut on I70. I can't tell you much due to client confidentiality but since your family owns the place you need to know what might happen."

Without disclosing identifying information, Lauren filled Bryan in about Penny's planned meeting on Saturday with her online friends. She emphasized it could be entirely innocent but due to the increased rate of abductions recently in the state, Dr. Cheaney was speaking to his contacts at the state police.

Bryan was lost in thought for several seconds. "I've become so self-absorbed that I can't imagine anything like that could ever happen at one of our stores," he said. "I plan to be there myself on Saturday, to be sure nothing goes wrong."

Lauren tempered his anger and concern. "No, what you're going to do is follow whatever direction the state police give us," she said. "It may be better that you stay away."

"That's not fair, Lauren. You've told me something I have to respond to."

"Look, Bryan, just as I trusted your instincts to come up with a way to salvage your business, you have to trust me when it comes to my work. I'll let you know the minute I hear from Dr. Cheaney."

Just after she arrived at work the next day, Dr. Cheaney asked to see Lauren. She was to tell Penny and her mother that the meeting could proceed for Saturday but that police in plain clothes would be monitoring the situation at Burger Hut.

"Penny will be angry," Lauren said. "But Sheila will be very grateful for the protection and support if it's needed. They're checking in today, so this will preempt anything else they want to talk about."

To Lauren's shock, Penny was accepting of the plan. "Bobby has started to ask weird questions," Penny said. "He wanted to know if I could dress sexy and if I wore makeup. He said he likes his girls to look like girls. My purple hair was, actually, his idea. I know, I know. I lied to you about that. I'm sorry." Penny looked defeated, both physically and psychologically. Her hair, which now sported two-inch roots, had faded into a flat shade of lilac gray.

Lauren and Sheila looked at each other with raised brows. "His girls?" Sheila said archly. "Lauren, will you be at the restaurant too?"

"I can't be there," she responded. "The authorities

have prohibited me and the owner of the Burger Hut from being around. There's too much danger that you'll look at us, act uncomfortable, and give things away. But the police will do whatever needs to be done. Hopefully, that will be nothing. Probably Bobby will turn out to be a senior in high school with a macho attitude."

Now if she could just get Bryan to be so compliant. He resented being kept out of the action on Saturday but it would be better if he let the authorities do their jobs. She felt for him. He was working so hard to save his family's business that ignoring criminal activity at one of their restaurants went against his every instinct.

As it turned out, the event was over before it began. The state police had Bobby and his friend in cuffs before Penny, Tracy, and Sheila had left home. Lauren, who had been kept in the loop by the officer in charge, called Sheila before the trio left Gordon.

"Turns out Bobby is thirty-eight, has a record dating back a few years, and is wanted for the attempted abduction of a Plainfield girl last month," she reported to Penny and her mother, who had her on speakerphone. "He's been trying to break in to the trafficking industry for a while. Kind of a sick career path, huh? Anyway, as I've said to you two before, you make quite a team when you communicate with each other. You can add 'crime stoppers' to your list of achievements."

"Thanks, Lauren," Penny said tearfully. "How can I ever get involved with a guy again? I can't trust any of them. They're all scum!"

Sheila interjected and Lauren noted that she didn't play into Penny's drama. "Honey, you've got time on your side and plenty of boys at school for you to get to know. At your age, there's no need for this anonymous Internet meet-and-greet. The key to trusting men is to get to know them up-close and personal before you commit. This online stuff is too risky for you."

"Speaking for you, or me?" Penny asked.

"Both of us," Sheila shot back. "I'll admit I've dated some real cases recently. I've jumped into relationships way too early. I'm sorry for that. I realize now it was hard on you in ways I didn't imagine."

The call ended with Lauren feeling grateful all had gone well. The power of counseling was again brought home to her as she thought about the horrific things that could have happened to Penny if she had met Bobby on her own. Her belief in her chosen profession, despite its stress, was reinforced. She'd needed that validation for some time now and she had the peaceful realization she could be a therapist in many settings, not just at the clinic. Then she realized with a start that she needed to call Bryan to update him on the events at the Burger Hut.

When he answered, she was startled by the noise in the background. "Where are you Dawson? Did Mohr's call you in today?"

"Not Mohr's, the I70 Hut. Whenever there's police action, I get called. So there's no need to fill me in. I got to read the police report. I've already talked to Dad about our security and about training our servers to be alert for signs of human trafficking. He, like me, had no idea that the sex-trade was hitting so close to home. Maybe Dr. Cheaney's contact at the state police could help us out with training."

She didn't mention it but Lauren noted that Bryan had called his father "Dad" during their conversation. She thanked God for all that He was doing in Bryan's life. And she thanked Him for keeping Penny and Tracy safe.

As she thought about the potential tragedy that had been avoided today, her sense of peace grew stronger. Being fearful did no good. Trust in God's protection was the key. And for the second time in recent months, she felt convicted. Why not trust Bryan and believe that God would protect her if needed? What was she afraid of? That he would cheat? That he would leave her for a woman with money? That he would tire of her principles? She shook her head as these thoughts tried to take hold. She had proven she could come through such abandonments intact. God had helped her when Doug betrayed her and He would continue to help her when needed. It was time to live her faith, to "walk the talk" as she told her clients.

Bryan got home late Saturday afternoon. He wondered why a just God would allow people to abduct innocent children for their own financial and sexual pleasure. It made no sense to believe in a loving God if He would allow such pain to occur in the world He created. Lauren sure believed in God. She would say God created us with free will with the capacity to love and to sin. He still couldn't buy in.

But he couldn't ignore Lauren's faith. It seemed to ground her, even when she was uncertain or off-balance. Her quiet belief in God's work permeated everything she did. She was a loving daughter, a steadfast friend, and a caring counselor. Suddenly, he wanted her to be a loving partner to him, as well. The realization hit him like a runaway train. He wanted Lauren in his life, all the time. He wanted her to be his friend, his partner, and his wife.

For the first time, he was struck by his total commitment to Lauren. Her understated beauty hid her inner strength and passion for life. Her grit in handling the predator case, her willingness to stand up to him when he wanted to be at the Burger Hut when the arrest came down and her love for others made him ache to be a permanent part of her life. But how would he convince her? How could he explain this jumbled mess of emotion?

Chapter Fourteen

Mondays at the mental health center were always unpredictable. This particular Monday was even more so. At the morning huddle, during which the on-call therapist updated clinicians on events of the weekend, Dr. Cheaney asked for extra time to speak at the end of the meeting. Wary of what was to come, staff members listened closely.

"As you've all been informed, the regional organization will be shifting soon, due to the closure of two smaller centers. This necessitates a change in our leadership. I'll be based in Indianapolis and a new director has been appointed for the Gordon office. Ricky Delphin, our senior social worker, has graciously accepted the position and all of the responsibility that comes with it. I expect you all to continue to work as the utmost professionals you are and to help her as she transitions into her new role."

A barely detectible pause occurred before Lauren led the group in polite applause. Ricky stood, smiling broadly, and thanked Dr. Cheaney for his support.

"I am thrilled to take on this task," Ricky said. "It's obvious that changes in our center are long overdue and I will look forward to everyone's input as they take place." As always, Ricky had a layer of perspiration on her upper lip and a rosy flush on her cheeks. The group of therapists looked at her in shock.

Dr. Cheaney also looked a bit taken aback but smiled politely as he clapped for Ricky. Lauren's worst fears were beginning to take shape. She couldn't believe that Ricky would insult Dr. Cheaney and his years of leadership so soon after being made director and in his presence to boot. Maybe her dream of private practice was going to be less a dream and more of a reality soon.

One thing at a time, she thought, taking a calming breath. Do your best work and let God help you figure out the next step.

After the group dispersed to meet with their first appointments of the day, Ricky called to Lauren. "If you've got a second, I'd like to talk," Ricky commanded.

"Sure, Ricky," Lauren said. "I've got to do case supervision with the IU master's student but he can review his tapes until I get there."

"Dr. Cheaney told me you declined his offer to be director," Ricky began. "I hope that we can work together now that I'm your boss. I respect your clinical work though, now that I'm director, your case notes will be reviewed as will those of the other therapists."

"Of course," Lauren said smoothly. Inside she was churning. Dr. Cheaney's practice had been to review randomly selected charts of all cases in the center and to trust his therapists to inform him of their difficulties or uncertainties. She wondered how in the world Ricky would have the time to review everyone's notes each week. With eleven clinicians on staff, she would be reading notes full-time, allowing no openings for her to see patients herself.

But maybe that's her goal, not to see patients. She's always so cynical at staffing. I've been worried about burnout but she's way ahead of me. And she's also into power and second-guessing. Terrific combination. Lauren's thoughts spiraled downward as she looked at Ricky.

Ricky continued. "I have the greatest respect for Dr. Cheaney as you know, Lauren. But he ran quite a loose ship. I won't be liable for cases about which I know nothing. He told me about the situation at the Burger Hut and, though I supported your decision-making while he and I talked, I was appalled at your delay in informing him of the mess Sheila allowed Penny to get into."

Staring at Ricky, Lauren again drew deep, even breaths. She thought of puppies, the crown jewels, and her beloved dining room suite, but nothing helped. She wanted to give Ricky her opinion of Ricky's skills. No, she wanted to call Ricky a fraud, a poser, and worse. Finally, after a quick prayer, she responded to Ricky's snide assessment of her clinical work.

"Actually, Dr. Cheaney commended my handling of that case," Lauren said, with a smile pasted on her face. "He made it clear if Penny were pushed too early in treatment, she would leave therapy. I believe that was an accurate assessment. But, I realize in our profession everyone has a different supervisory style. Thanks for giving me the heads up about yours."

Ricky peered at Lauren closely, clearly suspicious of the younger woman's meaning. "Nonetheless, Lauren, my new role is the culmination of all I've hoped for professionally. For many years, I've considered leaving the center for a private practice. Obviously, only do-gooders intent on working for almost minimum wage go down that road these days."

She paused, expecting Lauren to respond. Lauren sat calmly, waiting for more.

"Well, I guess that's it then. Have a good day, Lauren."

"Will do. You do the same, Ricky."

Her day could only get better from here on. Was Ricky hinting that she should resign? Or had Dr. Cheaney told Ricky about her eventual goal of having a practice of her own? Neither possibility was good.

The day progressed quietly, in spite of its ragged beginning. Unlike usual Mondays, when therapists and case managers would have eaten their sack lunches together, joking about their weekends, everyone ate at their desks with their doors closed. Obviously, the atmosphere had already taken on Ricky's stamp – serious, defensive, and isolated.

Lauren longed to process the morning's meeting with Dr. Cheaney but he left for the main office immediately after it ended. It was time to be a big girl, to decide her own fate. She could work for Ricky and use the time to build up her savings before she went out on her own. Or not.

As she thought about her uncertain professional future, Kristen tapped on her door. "Come on in," Lauren said, forcing a smile.

"I wanted to thank you for talking to me the other day," Kristen said. "Afterwards, it struck me that you sounded a lot like Dr. Cheaney. Good input without being condescending. Unlike Ricky, for the record."

"I'm glad if I helped," Lauren said, ignoring the opening to talk trash about Ricky. No sense in burning bridges so early in the game. "How have things been going?"

"Better, I think. I'm more relaxed with my clients when I'm able to be myself. And when I'm relaxed, I listen and think better. I only had one cancellation last week and it was due to the flu that's going around the high school."

"Good for you! You're a good counselor, Kristen. Hang in there."

"Also, I broke up with my boyfriend," Kristen continued. "Turns out he was the one who liked me in all black. Can you believe I fell for that?"

"Been there, done that, in a different relationship," Lauren said with meaning. "But things will get better in that area, too. Trust me."

"You do seem happier lately," Kristen observed. "Care to tell me his name?"

"Too soon to share details," Lauren said. "Or maybe I'm just afraid of jinxing it!"

"Well, if he has a single brother, keep me in mind," Kristen said with emphasis. "I don't want to give up on men due to one disappointing relationship. Life is too short to close that chapter."

Lauren watched in stunned silence as Kristen

left her office. Unlike Kristen, she had been ready to give up, without a doubt. Even now, after Bryan's impressive work at Mohr's indicating both business savvy and devotion to his family, she couldn't bring herself to open up to him completely. What if he saved the business and then had no use for her? Or what if he couldn't save the business and dropped her for a more successful woman? She was angry with herself for revisiting these old thoughts. God would protect and strengthen her. Maybe Kristen, a self-professed agnostic, had more faith than she did!

Bryan's Monday was filled with glitches as well but, as part owner of Mohr's, he didn't need to worry about anyone firing him. If he lost his job, it would be his own doing. The constant meetings with his father, uncle, and cousin drained him, but the changes planned for Mohr's survival were coming along. He missed Lauren's sweet support, so he called her the minute he felt she would be free of the center.

"Hey, you," he said happily. "Let's have a Monday feast. How about a steak? Not sure how much longer I'll be able to afford that, so let's live large."

"Not funny," Lauren moaned. "I'll be on my ramen noodle diet sooner than you think, buddy. Ricky thinks I bungled the Burger Hut case despite Dr. Cheaney's praise and she has me under her microscope. If I don't leave soon, either I'll be demoted to doing case management or I'll be fired for insubordination when I spout off about her nasty philosophy of adolescent psychology."

After hearing about Lauren's day, Bryan issued an executive order, one he had been aching to make. "No talk of work allowed at our Monday feast," he declared. "It's time we talk about us."

Lauren's stomach clenched as she dressed for dinner. What did "talk about us" mean? Was he going to end their relationship, or whatever it was, now that the wedding was over and his business was on track? Her worst fear had been that he would find someone else. A woman with money, a business background, comfort with casual sex. A woman not like her, in other words. Maybe that had happened after all.

Help me, dear Lord. I'm going to trust you but it's hard. I know I'll be okay whatever happens, with your grace and support. Trusting God was certainly a challenge for her. She was praying the same prayer all the time!

Bryan picked Lauren up and they drove in silence to the steak house. Lost in her thoughts, she wondered why Bryan was quiet. But then again, he had forbidden talk of their jobs, so what did that leave them to discuss? Was their relationship based solely on their problems at work?

Each of them had dressed for a special occasion. Bryan was in his navy suit while Lauren wore a short, swingy tent dress that accentuated her petite frame and toned legs. Despite their festive attire, to the casual observer, they probably looked miserable and anxious.

After they were seated and had placed their orders, Lauren began.

"I'm a little concerned," she admitted. "What did you mean when you said we needed to talk about us?"

Bryan smiled the smile that always soothed her heart while also causing it to skip a few beats. His blue eyes sparkled with mischief. "I hoped you'd be off balance," he teased. "You're always calling me out on my defenses and now it's my turn. Here goes. Why do you call me 'Dawson' or 'mister' or 'buddy' so often? Just like when you said calling my parents by their first names was a way to stay distant from them, I think you should be using my name, or terms of endearment, when we talk. I prefer 'darling' and 'sweet cakes,' by the way."

Lauren blushed and looked down at her heavy china plate. "Well done, Bryan," she said quietly. "You're right, I keep you at arm's length sometimes. It feels safer to me."

"What's unsafe about me?" Bryan asked heatedly. "I'm not Doug, or a guy on the prowl for sex, despite what you think. I really care for you, Lauren. When we're not talking, I find myself wanting to touch base, just to hear your voice."

"I didn't mean to upset you," Lauren said. "For the record, I find myself wanting to talk to you all the time, too. It's just that since Doug and I split up, I've gotten used to relying on myself for everything. That's what feels safe, instead of trusting you. I know that's unfair. But I tell my clients to allow themselves to heal at their own pace, which is what I think I'm doing."

"Maybe, maybe not," Bryan said. "When will you know you're healed if you can't take a risk and trust a man? That's part of healing, in my non-psych opinion. If you had a broken leg, you'd take the risk of walking with the cast and crutches, right? And after the cast was off, you'd jump back into life as if nothing had happened. But you would know to be cautious on the ski slopes, so to speak. I think you're being too careful. You've given up skiing and you're missing out on lots of happiness."

Lauren looked at Bryan closely. He seemed sincere. He made good points, despite his messy ski metaphor. But he was almost too handsome and charming and that struck her for the first time. Was she hesitating because he was so attractive he could have anyone he wanted, like Doug had? But his words contradicted such fears and, certainly, Doug had never been so open and vulnerable with her. Doug's idea of intimate conversation had been discussing Tiger Woods's latest back surgery and its implications for the FedEx golf cup standings.

"I agree, I think," she said. "Boy, I wish we could talk about work. It would be easier than this."

The wait staff arrived at that moment with their food. Conversation was at a minimum for the next several minutes. Each of them complimented the tender filets and Lauren took the opportunity to thank Bryan for such an expensive meal.

"You're welcome," he said testily. "But Lauren, there's no one else I'd rather take out for a meal, whether it be for steak or a dollar burger. There's no one I'd rather do anything with, actually. You still don't think I'm committed to you, do you?"

Bryan's pressured argument continued. "You're always talking about faith, giving things to God, and accepting His plan. I've tried to get on board with that and to be honest, the crisis at Mohr's has renewed what little faith I had in God. My family has gotten closer and we all have a sense that whatever happens will be for the best. I can only attribute that to God's intervention in our lives. I've been praying each night, in praise, in thanksgiving, and in request for forgiveness. Just like I learned back in Sunday school. You're the first person I've told about that. Again, there's no one else I'd share that with."

"But what about your faith, Lauren?" Bryan asked pointedly. "Don't you think that God has brought us together for a reason – that for us to be a couple is part of His will?" Bryan paused for a breath and waited for Lauren's response.

She thought about all of her prayers since her broken engagement to Doug. She remembered wondering if God meant for her calling to be as a single woman. And she realized Bryan was His response to her prayers. Suddenly, she believed in miracles. Bryan was her miracle but she hadn't been able to see that until he called her out on her faith.

"My faith is good but not as strong as yours!" she said, trying to calm her pounding heart. "You're right, Bryan. We were meant to be. I thank all that is holy that you figured it out because I'm not sure if I ever would have!"

Before she lost her nerve, she pressed on. "I'm sorry I've been so slow to trust you. It's not only about Doug, either. My cautious way of living, my need for control, and my focus on frugality to the point of stinginess, they all result in me closing off from the world. It's too easy for me to stay in all weekend stewing in the silence and then go to work on Monday still tired and spent. My world with you would be different but that's a good thing, Bryan. You seize life, no matter what it hands you."

"I have things to be sorry for too," Bryan said with a loving gaze. "I didn't respect how important having a true relationship was to you. I assumed your history with Doug was the reason for everything that went wrong between us. It was easy for me to turn him into a scapegoat, rather than looking at my own past. My relationship with Angela progressed much too quickly and I leaned on her because I felt out of my element in the MBA program. I'm only now realizing how much it hurt when she wouldn't come back to Gordon with me. You've shown me what a real loving partnership can be."

They left the restaurant holding hands. At Lauren's house, they had coffee and sat in contented silence as they thought about their feelings for each other. Bryan finally broke the happy quiet.

"I love you, Lauren. I haven't said those words nearly enough. Actually, the one time I said them, it was begrudgingly. You are everything to me. I want to be with you forever. What about a wedding? When is the earliest we can get married?"

"Is that an actual proposal?" Lauren asked, truly surprised. "If so, I accept!"

"Of course it's a proposal," Bryan said smoothly, bringing her back to reality. "But I don't have the ring with me. That will have to wait until tomorrow. I hope you're okay with a family heirloom. You're the frugal one in this relationship but at present I have limited cash to spend on a big rock."

"I'd be okay with a thin gold wedding band," she replied, her eyes glistening. "My mom's all about the bling, not me. But I'm glad my frugal nature is taking hold of you. More importantly, I need to kiss my fiancé."

"You haven't said it yet," Bryan noted when he came up for air.

"Said what? I accepted your proposal, despite its unromantic wording," Lauren said with a smile. Then she realized what he meant.

"I love you, Bryan Dawson. I haven't said it enough either, although I've thought it lots of times. You've taught me so much about life and living. I love the dogged way you looked for solutions to save Mohr's. I love your stubborn nature as evidenced by your refusal to listen to the expert consultants. I love that you can look at your parents with understanding, not resentment. I love that you insisted staff at your restaurants have training about human trafficking. I love your family and I love being in your arms. I love the idea of all that will follow the smooching after we're married! Is that what you wanted to hear?"

"Perfect," Bryan said. "That's exactly what I needed to hear."

After more kissing, their evening ended early. Bryan called his parents with the news as he drove home. Tom answered, was happy for his son and when Sally overheard the gist of the conversation, she insisted on talking to Bryan.

"Honey, this is wonderful," she gushed. "Lauren is an amazing woman. You two will be a great couple."

"Thanks, Mom," he said. "Can I stop by tomorrow and get Grandma's sapphire ring for Lauren? You said once that it was mine when the time came. I think Jeff got her ruby band to give to Mandy, right?"

"Of course you can have the sapphire," Sally said. "That ring will be perfect for Lauren. Elegant, classy, and understated."

"Thanks for all you've done to help smooth the way with Lauren, Mom," Bryan said. "I'm just now realizing how good you are at planting seeds without seeming to meddle."

"Who, me?" Sally asked innocently. "Haven't a clue what you mean, son. We'll see you and Lauren tomorrow for supper."

Lauren's parents were equally positive when she phoned them.

"Sweetie, we're thrilled," Janice said. "Your dad and I couldn't have asked for a better man to have as our new son. I've been able to gauge your relationship peaks and valleys in the last few months. Hopefully, you're going to be happier now! Please come by for dinner this weekend when we can take our time to get better acquainted with Bryan."

Peter took the phone from Janice, happy but tentative about Lauren's news. "Honey, what I know about Bryan Dawson is all good but I've also noticed he can bring you down. Are you sure about this? Do you want to give it a little more time before you say you'll marry him?"

"No, Dad, he's great," Lauren insisted. "A lot of my sad times were related to getting over Doug and growing up a little when it came to relying on God. Bryan is nothing but the best for me."

Despite the pressure of their jobs, Tuesday was a more relaxed day for both Bryan and Lauren. He was able to navigate meetings with architects, bankers, and publicists with ease. Mohr's new identity was taking shape and given the smooth way the planning phase was going, the store would be reopened in early May.

Lauren dealt with an array of clients and she ignored Ricky's arched brow after running a few minutes late after a particularly complex session. She hoped her husband-to-be would continue his newly-found frugality because it was obvious she would be working for herself pretty soon. She'd managed on a small income before and she knew she could do it again. Surprisingly, she didn't feel anxious or alone. She knew Bryan would be supportive of her no matter what. His tenuous job situation didn't faze her either. Maybe her belief in God's will and provision was finally becoming stronger.

In response to that thought, Lauren made a quick trip to Sawyer's Furniture Store after work. Bryan had said Luke Sawyer helped him furnish his apartment, so Lauren asked Luke about a layaway account on new office furniture. She needed to put her plan for a private practice in motion just in case Ricky decided on the timing before she was ready.

"We offer layaway, Lauren," Luke said. "But you still have to commit to purchasing the furniture. There's no changing your mind before it's paid off. Are you ready to agree to that? And where are you going to put this stuff? Do you have a home office?" Luke knew Lauren worked at the mental health center and he was understandably confused.

"I'm thinking my home sewing room could serve a dual purpose. Right now, I'm using the dining room table as my bill-paying center," Lauren said. She hated fibbing to Luke but there was no sense in starting the Gordon gossip mill about her need for new furniture.

Luke gave Lauren a tour of the professional furniture inventory. She had a brief moment of panic, considering the amount of money that she was pledging toward a desk, two overstuffed chairs, a small loveseat, and a file cabinet.

I can do all things, with God's help, she thought. And Bryan's. I feel more at peace than I have in a long time. Don't I tell my clients that options are always good? Now I have lots of options!

Dinner at the Dawson lake house was fun, despite Lauren's nerves. Tom grilled marinated chicken breasts, which were accompanied by Sally's potato salad and relish tray. She proudly produced a chocolate "engagement cake" after the meal which was lopsided but tasty.

"Mom, this is wonderful," Bryan said. "You continue to surprise me."

"Wait until you see what I've got planned for our condo above Mohr's," Sally said. "I've been to salvage yards, flea markets, and discount houses. My decorating theme will be rustic Indiana, with a dash of our current furniture. The pieces need to be neutral enough to fit in. The rest of our things will be donated to the local Salvation Army."

Tom rolled his eyes but looked befuddled and happy. "Son, we've got ourselves two powerful women," he chuckled. "Buckle up for an exciting ride."

Bryan took Lauren out to the lakeside deck after dinner. As they looked at the stars reflecting off the inky water, he gave her his grandmother's ring, a royal blue sapphire with trillion-cut diamonds on each side.

"It's beautiful," Lauren said, looking into his eyes, which had deepened in color to match the stone. "But as I said, a gold band would make me just as proud." They kissed deeply until Bryan broke away.

"Now that we're official, when's the soonest we can get married?" he asked. "Are you going to make your dress? How long will that take? Do you want a big wedding or something more intimate and, therefore, more easily planned? I vote for the quicker, the better. There's no need to go crazy over the dress, like you did with Jenny's. It will be off soon enough," he said, wiggling his brows.

Lauren laughed at his not-so-subtle message. "Yes, I'm making my dress. No it won't take long. And having just close friends and family is how I've always envisioned my wedding. Good thing I know you better, Dawson, or I'd think you had ulterior motives for getting married quickly."

"I do have ulterior motives and you know it," Bryan laughed. "But the most important one is to have you with me all the time, so that I don't have to worry about scaring you off or making you angry. When we're married, you'll have to stay put. We can duke it out until things are settled."

"Or we can kiss and make up, instead of duking

it out," Lauren responded. "I agree that being together full-time will be nice."

"Nice? That's an interesting spin on newlywed
life," Bryan said as he pretended to be angry. "I can
think of other ways to describe a newlywed couple.
I think the British call it 'loved up,' or something
like that."

"So, to get down to specifics, are you thinking
next week, next month, next fall?" Bryan continued. "All this talk of what's to come is making me
antsy."

Lauren laughed. "Believe it or not, I'm as impa-
tient as you are, my love. How about an early April
wedding? That gives my mom and me enough time
to get things together. My dress will be simple but
classic. The only issue is location for the ceremony
and reception. Venues are booked a year in advance
around here."

"We're currently at the perfect place for a small
wedding," Bryan replied. "Mom and Dad offered
the lake house if we wanted it for the ceremony
and reception. Since we're not inviting hundreds of
people, the main floor will be more than adequate
to handle family and friends. If it's not too cold, we
can spread out to the deck for part of the time. In
fact, my brother Jeff and his wife were married in
front of the great room fireplace. We could start a
Dawson family tradition, except, duh, they're selling the house in May."

"So we'll give the house a romantic image for
the new buyers," Lauren said happily. "What better
selling point than 'ideal location for family weddings?'"

Epilogue

Lauren's layered tulle skirt shimmered as it reflected the light from the candles surrounding the massive fireplace. The gown, which she had made in a record two weeks, had a shirred bandeau top. The snug waistline was cinched with a satin ribbon belt featuring a large bow in the back. Aunt Abby's vintage crystal broach highlighted the center front of the sash, sparkling in blue stones that matched Lauren's engagement ring. Surprisingly, Lauren had focused not on the dress but on her love for Bryan as she cut and stitched the princess gown. What a contrast to the angst that she had felt as she fashioned Jenny's dress! She knew this dress was important but not nearly as crucial as the man she was about to marry and their life together. She had finally figured out her real priorities.

Lauren's veil, on loan from Jenny, and the prototype for one of the sample veils in the new line at Mohr's, was her "something borrowed." Her ring and broach satisfied both the "something old" and "something blue" requirements. Obviously, her dress was "something new."

A periwinkle, loose-fitting tea-length dress emphasized a hint of baby bump her matron-of-honor, Jenny, proudly sported. Little Courtney Stanfield wore a matching dress, absent the sequined "A-MA-ZIIING" she had insisted would be the perfect accent to the ribbon sash. Everything was perfect as Lauren and Bryan said their vows in front of their families and friends.

He kissed her at the end of the ceremony while the guests applauded. Looking deeply into her eyes, he whispered, "We're in this together, for better or worse. Between the changes at Mohr's, your new private practice, and all the kids we're going to have, we'll never be bored! I love you, honey."

Smiling, Lauren looked into her husband's eyes and said, "I love you, too, Dawson. As you reminded me once, I'm ready to jump back into life. We're going to have a great time!"

A Look at Book 2, Crafted With Love

A contemporary sweet romance story of small-town relationships, grief and reconciliation, and risking it all for love.

Sophie Sutliff is a delightful but challenging six-year-old. When Psychologist Kristen Anderson rescues the lost little girl at a 5k race, her father, Mike, practically charges Kristen with child abduction. Despite his good looks, Kristen in unimpressed with the new town hospitalist. She has plenty to keep her busy: three part-time jobs, a mother with health issues, and a goofy Labradoodle. There's no need to add a grumpy doctor and his cute daughter to the mix.

Despite a career as a successful physician, Mike feels like a failure in most areas of his life. His marriage has ended, his daughter splits her time between his home in Gordon and his ex-wife's in Indianapolis, and he's adjusting to working in a small-town hospital. Determined to take control of his life, Mike decides his next romance will be with a Proverbs-type woman who's nearly perfect and if he's honest, a bit subservient.

COMING MAY 2021

About Leanne Malloy

Born in Ohio and raised in Indiana, Leanne's writing reflects a midwestern sensibility and belief in God's love, grace, and provision. Her first job at age fifteen was at a chain fabric store, followed by careers as a dietitian and psychologist. Scenes from her novels therefore include sewing, crafting, and an emphasis on the mind-body connection. Leanne's Italian heritage, equating food with love and kinship, serves as a setting for other episodes in her books, as does her work with food pantries. Food as ministry resonates strongly with her.

A homebody at heart, Leanne's life is full provided there are family and friends in frequent contact, opportunities to travel, and books to be written.

About Leanne Malloy

CPSIA information can be obtained
at www.ICGtesting.com
Printed in the USA
BVHW041240220123
656770BV00003B/120

9 781647 345419